THE *Angel*
BETWEEN THEM

D0067505

A *Huron Cove* SERIES ROMANCE BY
ROB SHUMAKER

"And now these three remain:
faith, hope and love.
But the greatest of these is love."

1 Corinthians 13:13

CHAPTER 1

Huron Cove, Michigan

"Well, look what the cat dragged in." Arlene Cooper wiped her hands on a towel and watched with mild amusement at one of her favorite customers approaching the counter. "You look like you had quite the time last night."

Ethan Stone nodded his throbbing head once as he stopped at the counter of The Coffee Cove, Huron Cove's most trusted place for coffee, muffins, and cakes. Ethan didn't feel the need for baked goods this Friday morning—his stomach wasn't sure it could handle them. But the smell of fresh roasted coffee beans gave him hope that his day could take a turn for the better.

"Coffee, Arlene. Black coffee."

Arlene didn't know whether to smile at Ethan or shake her head at him. For starters, she grabbed the pot and poured him a piping hot cup. The motherly lecture might come later. "You doing okay?"

Ethan leaned his elbow on the counter and rested his head in his right hand. "I've got a pounding headache. I was hoping Huron Cove's finest coffee would help get me through the day."

Arlene handed over the cup. "You're going to have to get through the morning first."

Ethan took a sip and the caffeine gave him a quick jolt. He managed a smile, but not big enough to start the pounding in his head again. He vaguely remembered last night. There was a bar and loud music, at least he was sure of that. But how he wound up in his own bed was a mystery. Oh well, living life to the fullest.

"Haven't I warned you guys about your late-night carousing?" She took Ethan's money, punched some buttons on the cash register, and then gave him back his change. "One of these days it might catch up to you."

Ethan looked at her with his bloodshot eyes and heavy eyelids. "I think you might have mentioned it once or twice over the years." He and his buddies had been known to paint the town of Huron Cove red a time or two. Or maybe it was more than that. How many days of the week were there? Before he could take another sip, the bell over the opening door announced a new customer with a tinny clang.

"There's the man," Curt Conrad said, spying Ethan at the cash register and clapping his hands.

Ethan cringed and his hand shot up to his forehead. "Not so loud."

"How about a coffee, Arlene?" Curt said. He slapped Ethan on the back just to rub it in. "Ol' Ethan and I had quite the time last night. Didn't we?"

Ethan took another sip and blinked. "I'm not sure I remember that much, Curt."

"Hah! That's okay. I've got videos on my phone to remind you!" Curt pulled out his phone and tapped the screen a couple times to bring last night's memories back to life. Once the video started playing, he turned the screen so Arlene could enjoy the show.

"I'm going to go stand over there," Ethan said, taking his coffee and his dignity to the other end of the counter.

Ethan Stone was Huron Cove's most eligible bachelor, living a life where he worked hard, played hard, and had a good time doing both. Many thought it would be next to impossible to tame this bucking bronco. There was no shortage of women in town who would love nothing more than to have the hunky Ethan sweep them off their feet and whisk them off to a land of wedded bliss. But being the gentleman he was, he probably would have told them that marriage was the last thing on his mind.

Having the love of your life dump you for all of Huron Cove to see had a way of scarring one for life. And even though it had been almost two years, he still hadn't gotten over losing Olivia Daniels. He thought she was the one. How wrong he was.

After some shrieks of laughter from Arlene and the faint sound of some country western music, along with some high-pitched "yee-haws" coming from his phone, Curt grabbed his coffee and headed for a stool next to his buddy. They had been best friends since the day they met in kindergarten, and the constant ribbing was all a part of the friendship that lasted through high school, college, and their time as adults in Huron Cove.

"Sorry about that," Curt said, although he didn't sound too apologetic. He took a seat on the stool. "But that was too good not to show off."

"Thanks, I appreciate that, bud. At least you didn't put it up on the Internet."

Curt took a sip. He apparently didn't suffer the same aftereffects as Ethan. "Whattya got going on today?"

Ethan took a moment to remember what day it was. Friday. He guessed that was why he wasn't still in bed. Maybe tomorrow. "I've got to mow the fields and tend the orchard. Cherry season is in full bloom. And then it's over to Mrs. Sanderson's house and a couple more yards after that."

With his black jeans and blue button-down shirt, Ethan

Stone was ready for business. Having been the boss of his family's landscaping business for almost three years now, he had to look and dress the part when he was in town on errands. But, given that the business was having trouble keeping its doors open, he would have to switch shirts and get his hands dirty before nine a.m.

The late spring and summer months were prime growing season for central Michigan. Known as one of the best produce growing grounds in the entire world, there was no shortage of need in tending to the cherries, blueberries, and apples that ripened throughout the state. Just west of Lake Huron on Michigan's Sunrise Coast, Huron Cove provided fruit lovers across the country with all sorts of goodness. But it took labor to get all of it to the customers.

"How is business by the way?"

"Business is business," Ethan said, eyeing his coffee cup. He grimaced and shook his head. "But I don't know if it'll be good enough to keep the homestead much longer."

"That tough?"

"With the economy the way it is, the bigger jobs aren't so big any longer. I have to take every little thing just to get by. The bills are starting to pile up. Luckily, it's just me. I don't know what I'd do if I had a family with multiple mouths to feed." He blew out a breath. "I'm hoping the summer will bring better opportunities."

Curt heard a buzzing sound coming from Ethan's shirt pocket. Perhaps his friend's senses were so dulled from last night that he didn't realize his phone was ringing. After about ten seconds, he asked, "Are you going to get that?"

Ethan pulled out the phone and looked at the screen. "I don't know who keeps calling me. It's an Ann Arbor number that I don't recognize. Probably a bill collector or somebody wanting money." He swiped the screen, silenced the buzzing, and put the phone back in his pocket. "If it's so important, they can leave a message. There ought to be a way to block these people."

Curt slapped him on the arm. "Hey, I forgot to tell you, I heard it through the grapevine that Olivia was coming back into town. Any truth to that?"

Ethan felt like a lightning bolt zapped him right between the eyes. He would have felt better if Curt had surprised him with a punch to the gut. Why'd he have to bring her up? Hadn't he told his best bud a thousand times that he didn't want to hear the name Olivia Daniels mentioned in his presence any longer. Olivia Daniels was officially off limits. Now and forevermore.

Curt looked over at Ethan, who was staring blankly into the black abyss of his coffee cup. "Did you hear me?"

"Yeah, I heard you. How would I know whether she's coming back to town?"

"I heard her dad wasn't doing so good."

Ethan shrugged. "I wouldn't know."

"What do you mean? Her parents live right next door to you."

"I don't get over there much anymore."

Curt had the decency to lower his voice so Arlene and the other patrons couldn't eavesdrop. "You got to get over her, man."

Ethan scowled and pointed a finger at him. "Hey, I am over her. She up and left and didn't look back. I'm not looking back either."

Curt shifted in his seat and leaned toward Ethan. "Is that why you can't seem to find yourself a good woman."

Ethan gritted his teeth. "This conversation is over."

Curt raised his eyebrows at Ethan's intensity and drank

down the rest of the coffee. Ethan could tell him a million times that he was over Olivia Daniels, but Curt knew better. Ethan and Olivia had been inseparable since grade school. High-school sweethearts whom everyone knew would someday tie the knot and have a houseful of beautiful kids. But somewhere, the fairy tale that was Olivia and Ethan went off the rails. Olivia left, and Ethan had been stuck in a rut ever since. One thing was for sure, Olivia Daniels was not going to break his heart again. No way, no how. They were never getting back together.

Ever.

Curt looked up at the TV. The morning news was in commercial, but Curt chuckled at what he saw. Fate had a way of slapping people upside the head just for the fun of it. He flicked Ethan on the arm and pointed to the TV.

"Hey look, there she is."

CHAPTER 2

Ethan turned his head just in time to find the beautiful blonde tresses of the woman he once loved more than anyone else on earth filling the TV screen. There she was for all the world to see—selling some newfangled brand of shampoo and conditioner that promised women everywhere that they too could look fabulous if only they raced to the store and forked over their money for a bottle.

Olivia Daniels had been one of Huron Cove's brightest stars. Valedictorian of her senior class and all-school most popular, she went on to become a cheerleader for the Big Blue at the University of Michigan in Ann Arbor. It was there that she took the acting classes with the hopes and dreams of becoming the next Jennifer Aniston.

Ethan took his eyes off the TV and gave a shake of his head. He had seen the commercial once before, and he didn't feel the need to be mocked by Olivia Daniels looking down at him. Would he ever be able to get over her? It was a little difficult considering he couldn't even turn on the TV without fear of seeing her selling shampoo or lipstick or mascara. Why couldn't she be relegated to selling fungal cream or extra-strength laxatives? Maybe then people around town wouldn't treat her like a goddess.

The commercial seemed to go on forever. What was it? A two-minute spot? By the end, an uncomfortable feeling washed over him. He couldn't help but wonder how many people in the coffee shop made the connection between the woman whose hair was blowing luxuriously in the wind and the man at the counter who mowed grass for a living. Most people avoided bringing up Olivia to Ethan, hoping not to dredge up bad memories.

The exception, of course, was Curt.

"Looking pretty good, huh?" With a big dumb grin on his face, he jabbed Ethan with an elbow. "Real good."

Ethan glared at him. "What is wrong with you? You remember what she did to me? You think it's funny or something?"

Curt caught the aggravation in Ethan's voice and held up his hands in surrender. "Hey man, I'm sorry. I'm just yanking your chain." Curt turned away to keep from laughing in Ethan's face, but what he saw out the window was just too much. *Oh man, could this day get any better?*

"Hey, Ethan, look." He pointed out the window. "There's Olivia right there."

Ethan looked out the window just in time to see Olivia's red Mustang slowly making its way down Main Street. With the warm summer weather and cloudless sky, she had the top down on the Mustang and the breezes blew her long blonde hair behind her. She looked like she could have been shooting a car commercial for Ford. Ethan groaned. The headache started pounding again.

"Told you she was coming back into town. You want me to run after her so you can say hello," Curt said, turning around on his stool to try and keep an eye on where Olivia was heading.

The two men saw the Mustang pull to a stop in a parking spot across the street. Once the car door opened, Olivia's long tanned legs stepped out and she walked down the sidewalk out of their view. Ethan let out a silent sigh, thankful that she hadn't headed to the coffee house. Maybe she was just in town for the weekend. If he was lucky, he might be able to avoid her if he took the back roads and kept to himself. It might be hard considering her family's bed-and-breakfast was located a stone's throw from Ethan's house. Maybe he would just shut himself inside, lock the doors for the next two days, and hope for the best.

Ethan thought he had better make his move quick so he asked Arlene for a refill to go. "I need to get to work," he told Curt.

His escape was thwarted when the bell announced the arrival of another customer. He turned away from the door, but the glimpse of radiant blonde hair in the mirror above the counter told him all he needed to know. Arlene confirmed it.

"Olivia Daniels!" Arlene hustled around the counter and opened her arms wide. "Huron Cove's Hollywood star!"

Olivia gave Arlene a big hug. Given the small-town atmosphere of Huron Cove, and the fact that Olivia had worked at the coffee house during her years at Huron Cove High, Arlene and Olivia had a long history of friendship.

"I don't know about Hollywood star, Arlene," Olivia said. "At least not yet."

A few of the regulars took notice of the commotion. Two women pointed and then whispered to the others at the table. The much-talked-about Olivia Daniels was in their midst.

"I'm so glad to see you. It's been so long," Arlene gushed. She pulled Olivia toward the counter and unleashed her questions. "You have to tell me all about it. Have you met George Clooney? What about Brad Pitt? Is Ben Affleck as tall as he seems on TV?"

Ethan still hadn't looked in Olivia's direction. Maybe she wouldn't notice him and that would give him an opportunity to escape. Thankfully, he had the world's greatest distraction machine at his fingertips. He turned his back to the two women and pretended to be fully engrossed in his cell phone. He glanced at the reflection of Olivia in the window. Even there she was beautiful. But now, he was cornered with no way out. There was no exit nearby. The best he could do was make like the potted plant against the wall and maybe bolt for the door once the coast was clear.

The sound of her voice hit his ears and traveled straight to his heart. So many thoughts started flooding his brain. She was the one. *Was* being the operative word.

Ethan decided he had to go. He had to get to work, but, in reality, he just needed to get out of there and as far away from Olivia Daniels as he could get. He didn't want to go through this again. He put the phone to his left ear and with the wall on his right, he headed to the opposite side of the coffeehouse. Acting completely absorbed with the nonexistent call on his phone, he didn't plan on stopping. *Don't look back. Don't stop for anyone. Just go.*

"Ethan, hi," Olivia said, grabbing him by the arm just steps from the door. She had asked Arlene to excuse her for a second to say hello to her old friend. "Were you just going to leave without saying hello?"

Ethan turned in time for the wave of Olivia's strawberry-scented fragrance wash over him. Probably the same stuff she'd been hawking on TV. The scent brought back a whole host of memories—some good, some bad—and his heart rate spiked. He remembered holding her in his arms, resting his head on hers as he took in the smell of her golden locks. But that was then, and this was now.

"I have to get to work."

* * *

Olivia noticed he didn't say hi. She also noticed he didn't look her in the eye. Even with the warm summer day, she could feel the frosty air between them. But the flood of memories wasn't felt by Ethan alone. His deep voice sent tingles down her spine just like when she was madly in love with him. The man she once loved seemed more handsome than she remembered. The square jaw was the same and the dark eyes could still make a woman's heart flutter. His skin was tan from working outdoors, and the tightness of his button-down shirt indicated he was not shy about manual labor.

"I'm just in town for a few days."

Ethan nodded. He took a step toward the door. "Okay."

"My dad isn't doing well."

"So I've heard."

"Maybe I'll stop by the house later and we can catch up."

"I'm going to be pretty busy this weekend, Olivia. I might not be around."

Olivia reached out her hand and placed a gentle touch on Ethan's forearm. "I'm sorry, Ethan. I don't want it to be awkward between us. We've known each other forever. We can still be friends, can't we?"

He ran his fingers through his dark hair and took a step back. "I really need to get to work, Olivia."

She wasn't going to fight it today. She didn't want to make a scene. Ethan pulling away from her made it clear he was uncomfortable. Maybe their friendship was beyond repair—a thing of the past.

"Okay. It was good seeing you again, Ethan."

* * *

Ethan offered a single nod to acknowledge Olivia and walked out the door. He had made the mistake of looking into her baby blue eyes. Those same eyes that he had dreamed about for so many years. The eyes that once looked at him lovingly and showed him how much she loved him. Or maybe they had been lying to him all that time.

His heart pounded in his chest, and his jaw hurt from the constant clenching. He thought he had moved on. The broken heart had begun to heal. And now? It was like the bandage had been ripped off and salt poured into the wounds. The pain and anguish was coming back to him. He didn't want to go through this again. *Don't look back. Don't stop for anyone. Just go.*

But he could feel his willpower faltering. The love of his life was in the building just behind him. She had meant everything to him. Just fifty feet and a glass window separated him from the woman of his dreams. *Don't look back. Don't stop for anyone. Just go.* His mind and heart raged in an epic struggle, a battle of wills that threatened to leave him senseless. *Don't look back. Whatever you do, don't look back.*

Ethan shook his head. *Remember what she did to you.* His mouth was dry, and he could almost feel the despair bubbling up inside of him ready to burst. The woman he once believed God made for him was so close—for the first time in two years they were together. He wanted to look back. He ached to look back. *Don't do it.* He made it to his truck and reached for the door handle. It was then that his mind finally gave in to the temptations of his heart. He shook his head, totally disgusted with himself.

And then he looked back.

CHAPTER 3

The smell of cinnamon hitting her nose as she entered the door told Olivia that her parents had guests. The Huron Cove Bed-&-Breakfast was world renowned for its hospitality, quiet serene setting, and, perhaps most of all, its blueberry cinnamon coffee cake. There were few smells that brought back memories of home-sweet-home more than Olivia's mother's coffee cake.

"Well, look who's home," June Daniels said as her daughter entered the kitchen. She wiped the flour off her hands with a towel and gave Olivia a hug.

"Hi, Mom. It's good to be home."

Olivia put down her suitcase and took a seat on a stool at the kitchen counter as her mom went back to work.

"Did you just get into town?"

Olivia held up her coffee cup. "I had to make a quick stop in to see Arlene and get a cup. Where's Dad?"

Her mother took her eyes off the recipe card. "He's at the cottages. Our guests just left for a day of boating on the lake, so your dad's tidying up."

The Daniels had operated the Huron Cove B&B for two generations, and Michigan travel guides had referred to it as the state's premier place for vacations, weekend getaways, and weddings. With picturesque views of Lake Huron and the Huron Cove lighthouse, guests marveled at its beauty and routinely gave it five-star reviews.

"How's Dad doing?"

Mrs. Daniels tapped the cake pan on the counter to even out the batter and looked up at her daughter. She didn't want to answer.

"Mom, how's he doing?"

Mrs. Daniels distracted herself with the oven controls. She finally found the words. "Your father is a stubborn man, Olivia."

"The doctor said it wasn't a heart attack. That's good, isn't it?"

Her mother nodded. "I'm not sure it wasn't a heart attack. He's starting to slow down, Olivia. It's a lot of work to keep the B and B in operation. I can do the cooking. That's not a problem. It's a labor of love for me. But your dad has to look after the cottages, manicure the grounds, and get everything ready for the guests. Then there's the reservations, the advertising, dealing with the desires of guests. It's causing him a lot of stress."

Olivia felt a hollowness in her stomach. She had been away in California for two years and didn't realize the toll the B&B was taking on her father. Perhaps she was naïve to think the B&B would last forever or that her parents would be welcoming guests until the end of time. Or maybe she just didn't want to think of the mortality of life. She missed this place. Huron Cove was her home, and it always would be.

"I'm not sure how much longer he'll be able to do it."

"Why doesn't he hire someone to help him?"

Mrs. Daniels waved off the question. "Oh, you know how your father is, he thinks he can do everything. And you know how picky he is about things. Every blade of grass has to be perfect, every view has to be gorgeous. We're thinking about . . ."

The mother-daughter conversation was interrupted when the back door to the garage opened. The thumping of work boots told those in the kitchen that Mark Daniels had returned.

"Well, well, well," he said, taking off his gardening gloves. "Look who's here."

Olivia rose up off her stool, somewhat shocked at what she saw. Her dad looked ten years older than the last time she had seen him. He looked like he had lost weight, and the bags around his eyes gave him a wearied look. "Hi, Dad." She wrapped her arms around him. "It's so nice to see you again."

Mr. Daniels gave his daughter a big hug. "It's nice to see you too, Olivia." He stepped back to look her over. "You are looking as beautiful as ever. As beautiful as a Michigan sunset."

"Mark, here's your iced tea," Mrs. Daniels said, handing him a tall glass. "Why don't you sit down and rest a while."

Olivia took a seat and patted the stool next to her. After her dad took a refreshing sip, she asked, "How are you doing?"

Mr. Daniels sighed. "Keepin' busy. It's June so you know what that means. Lots of guests to take care of."

Olivia reached out her hand and touched her dad's forearm. "Are you too busy? Mom says the B and B is wearing you down."

Mark gave his wife a look. It wasn't a look of anger that his wife had spilled the beans as to their private conversations, it was more a look of resignation. It was true. The B&B was beginning to take a toll on his health. He didn't give her an answer, almost too ashamed to admit it.

"Why don't you hire some help, Dad? It's time you and Mom enjoy more of the fruits of your labor."

Mr. Daniels took a deep breath and pondered the right

words. "The B and B is part of our lives, darling. I can't imagine not being around it, but I think the time has come to find new owners. I won't be able to do it forever, and we might as well get out when we're on top."

Olivia's jaw dropped. Her mother hadn't mentioned the B&B might be on the market. Was that the only alternative? Where would she go when she returned to Huron Cove? Where would the only home she ever knew be then?

She looked at her mother and then back at her father. "You can't sell this place, Dad." Her voice pleaded with him. "It's so beautiful here—the lake, the orchard, the lighthouse. Our family has been so blessed."

Mr. Daniels shook his head. "We have been blessed, Olivia. But unless we can get some help on both the reservation and planning side, not to mention the maintenance aspect, I'm not sure we'll have much choice. The place won't be five-star if your mother and I have to continue doing everything. And I won't let it be anything but the best if our name is on the sign. It might be time to step away."

Mrs. Daniels walked over and put a caring hand on her husband's shoulder. She looked at Olivia and gave her more bad news. "Your father has already told the city council he's not doing the fireworks this year."

Olivia's mouth fell open. "You're canceling the Fourth of July? People love the fireworks on the lake. It's tradition!"

Mr. Daniels shook his head in resignation. "I'm afraid it's time, Olivia. It's too much work to handle the fireworks and the B and B."

"What about Audrey and Beth?" Olivia asked, mentioning her older and younger sisters. "Maybe they can help."

Mrs. Daniels answered this one for her husband. "We've thought about it, but with Audrey living in Grand Rapids and Beth away at school in Ann Arbor, it just wouldn't work. Even if they could help with the reservations, they still couldn't do much with the cooking and the lawn."

Mr. Daniels smiled. His daughters had loved helping to plan for the guests when they were growing up. But their B&B expertise focused more on decorating and cooking. "Unfortunately, I didn't raise my girls to mow the grass and trim the bushes."

Olivia couldn't return the smile. Maybe he should have taught them instead of doing all the work himself. She couldn't believe what she was hearing. And a part of her couldn't believe what she was about to say.

"Maybe I could run the B and B."

CHAPTER 4

Mr. Daniels let out a laugh that reverberated around the kitchen. The laugh was a bit too long and too loud because he failed to see the tears forming in his daughter's eyes, her feelings hurt at her father's response. She was serious. When he finally realized that she meant what she said, he quieted down. Still, he didn't lie to make her feel better.

"Olivia, you can't run this place."

Olivia shrugged her shoulders and held out her hands, palms up. "Why not?"

Mr. Daniels looked at his wife and then cleared his throat. "Well, for starters, you're an actress living in California. The B and B is not a long-distance business. It's hands-on right here in Huron Cove, Michigan."

"I think I could do it," Olivia said, trying to hold back her tears. "I don't want you to sell our home."

Her father sighed. "Sweetie, let me see your hands." Olivia reached out both of her hands and he took them in his. "Look at these beautiful hands. They probably haven't seen a speck of dirt under the nails since you were in grade school." He raised his hands to the ceiling. "This is a twenty-four-hour operation. Seven days a week for most of the year. I don't think you can do it from Hollywood."

It was then that Olivia broke down in tears. The painful sobs indicated she wasn't just upset about the B&B. There was something else entirely, something that was breaking her heart and causing the tears to stream down her cheeks. She covered her face with her beautifully manicured hands.

Her father stood up and wrapped his arms around his daughter. "I'm sorry, honey. I didn't mean to make you cry. We're not selling the place today."

Mrs. Daniels walked around the counter and put her arm around Olivia. "Sweetie, what's wrong?"

Olivia sniffled back the deluge of tears and coughed. "I think I want to move back home."

"What?" her dad asked. "Why? What about your acting career?"

Olivia wiped away the tears streaking her cheeks with her hands. She needed to unload a ton of baggage that had been piling up in her heart for months now. "I haven't had an acting job in nearly a year."

"What? What are you talking about?" her mother asked. "We just saw you on TV the other day."

"That was an old show. I finished the filming of that episode last July. They finally got around to getting it on air."

Her dad reached out and patted her hand. How was she surviving without a job? He didn't ask that question. At least not yet. "Well, what have you been doing since then?"

"I've been going to a lot of auditions, but I haven't gotten anything. Not even a commercial." She started crying again. "And Gerard left me!" she wailed.

"Oh, sweetie, I'm so sorry to hear that." Her mother's hug grew tighter as Olivia sobbed with all her might. Her career was in shambles, and her beau had dropped her like a bad habit.

"I never did like that guy," Mr. Daniels snapped before he caught the daggers from his wife. *Probably not the right time, Dad.*

But it was true. Olivia had met Gerard Cologne (if that

was his real name) while in the theater department at the University of Michigan. He was middle age, brash, full of himself, and full of promises to a handful of young women in his acting class. Nearly twenty years older than most of his pupils, he took supreme interest in his "best student," the one he said was going to be a star. Olivia had fallen for him and the sweet French nothings he whispered into her ear when they canoodled after rehearsals.

Against her parents' wishes to finish school, Olivia hitched her wagon to Gerard and headed west—to the bright lights of Hollywood, the city of a thousand dreams. With some connections, Gerard had gotten Olivia some bit parts in a sitcom and a couple of commercials. But that was the best he could do. She had the looks of a supermodel, but her acting chops weren't Oscar worthy. She wasn't bad. There were just other actresses who were better. Although he promised to work with her to grow her talent, he quickly found a different star to latch onto. She was just as beautiful, and more importantly, she was more than willing to satisfy Gerard's every desire—something Olivia refused to do. Olivia Daniels would never compromise her principles, even if it meant missing out on her dreams. She was raised better than that, and God was first in her life. But in the cutthroat world of Hollywood, purity was not often rewarded.

"Sweetie, what happened?"

Olivia's tears quickly dried as she spat out her ex-boyfriend's name again. "Gerard's a jerk. He dumped me for someone else. He said he would love me forever but . . .," she said before her voice trailed off.

"Why didn't you tell us?" Mr. Daniels asked.

Olivia shook her head. "I wanted to, but I didn't want to admit my failure. He didn't love me for who I am. I know that now after he dumped me for Joy Masters."

"The new actress on *CSI*?" her mom asked.

Olivia nodded. Luckily, her mother didn't say how much she liked Masters in her new role.

"Olivia, you'll never be a failure to us," her dad said. "Acting is a hard business to get into. You have succeeded beyond our wildest imaginations. Everybody in Huron Cove tells us when they see you on TV. We're so proud."

"Thanks, Dad. But I think it's time I start looking for something more meaningful in life. Maybe acting will be a part of my future, but I don't like going from audition to audition and then waiting for the phone to ring. I need to do something productive."

Mrs. Daniels stood next to her husband and asked, "So what's next?"

"During my free time out in L.A., I took classes in event and wedding planning. It's something I've always loved."

Her mother agreed. "You were always my biggest helper when it came to setting up for the weddings we used to have here."

"I think that's what I'd like to do. I want to come home. I want to see the B and B thrive for another generation. I want to start holding weddings again. And I want the fireworks on the Fourth of July just like always."

Mrs. Daniels rubbed her hand up and down her husband's back and they looked into each other's eyes. Neither of them really wanted to sell the place. It had too many memories for them and their family. They didn't want to move to Florida or travel the globe. They had their very own piece of paradise right there on the Sunrise Coast of Michigan.

"What do you think?" Mrs. Daniels asked him.

Her husband took a few seconds to think of his answer. "Well, I love the idea of you coming back to help us,

Olivia. But the B and B isn't just a vacation and wedding destination. There's a lot more that goes into making this place beautiful. How are you going to keep everything in tip-top shape when I can't be of as much help in the future?"

"I'll figure it out, Dad. I promise. I really want to do this."

Mrs. Daniels suddenly had an epiphany. "Maybe you could ask Ethan to help out around here."

Olivia's eyes widened when she heard the name Ethan. Her parents hadn't mentioned his name in her presence in several years. But wasn't he the guy who just acted like he wanted nothing to do with her? Her mom was right, though. Ethan would be a huge help on the outdoor part of the B&B. He had helped her dad when Ethan was her boyfriend. But now. Could she really hire Ethan? Would he even accept?

"I don't know if he'll go for it, Mom. I think he's still bitter about what happened."

Mr. Daniels stood up. His rest was over, and it was time to get back to work. "Well, Olivia, all I can tell you is that Ethan Stone is the best landscaper in the area. Plus, he knows this place like the back of his hand." He stopped to plant a kiss on his daughter's forehead before heading outside. "If you want the B and B to continue in the family, Ethan Stone is the answer, if you ask me. I'll think about it some more, and then we can talk it over during dinner."

While her mother went back to checking on the coffee cakes, Olivia sat on the stool and looked outside to the green pasture to the north. When she turned her head to the right, she could see the stretch of sand fronting Lake Huron and the Huron Cove lighthouse in the distance. It wasn't Hollywood, and she didn't care. It was home. But for how much longer? She was going to have to become a businesswoman overnight and make the place shine.

And all it was going to take was asking for help from Ethan Stone—the man whose heart she crushed into a million pieces.

CHAPTER 5

The three knocks on the door were a little louder than normal, but Ethan knew Mrs. Sanderson's hearing wasn't what it used to be. Given the fact she was eighty-five-years old, he thought he should give her a few moments to shuffle to the door before knocking again. With no answer, he looked around the front of the house toward the garage. He thought she was home. She usually was on days when he mowed her lawn. Sometimes she would even sit out on the front porch with a pitcher of iced tea in case he was thirsty. Today, perhaps the ninety-five-degree heat of summer had kept her inside. Ethan raised his right hand to knock again but stopped when the curtain next to the door was pulled back. The white-haired woman's eyes widened and a broad smile formed on her face. She closed the curtain and turned the lock.

"Oh, it's my Ethan," she said after opening the door. "It's so good of you to stop by."

Ethan pulled open the storm door and stepped forward. "Hi, Mrs. Sanderson."

"Come in. Come in." She patted him on the forearm with her bony hand.

"I just finished up the yard," he said loudly.

Mrs. Sanderson turned slowly and glanced back out the living-room window. She didn't have to look at it very long. Ethan had been mowing her lawn for what seemed like ages, and he always did a wonderful job. "It looks lovely. Come into the kitchen so I can get you a glass of iced tea. It's so hot out there today, I have been staying cool in the air conditioning."

Ethan walked slowly behind her. He had been in the house a thousand times. It still looked the same as when he first starting mowing the Sandersons' yard when he was ten years old. The knickknacks were still in the same place—seashells from long forgotten trips to Florida, Precious Moments figurines from a host of life's milestones, and a praying hands statue of a regular churchgoer. The photos on the wall were the same too—her with her dearly departed husband, their children, as well as the grandchildren she rarely got to see.

Mrs. Sanderson opened the fridge and reached inside. "I just made a fresh pitcher."

With her distracted, Ethan gave a look at his watch and winced. He still had two more lawns to mow. He knew his time with his former grade school English teacher wasn't going to be short. But there was little he could do about it.

"Sit down, sit down," she said, motioning to him. Ethan took a seat on the white vinyl chair. The tall glasses were already on the table. "It's so good to see you, Ethan. It's seems the older I get, the fewer people come by to visit." She poured him a glass and then one for herself. "There we go."

Once she got settled in her seat and took a sip, Ethan asked, "How have you been doing?"

She smiled at his caring. He had been one of her favorite students, and then there was the lawn mowing. Ethan had started when Mr. Sanderson had grown too old to take care of the half an acre and, with the exception of some time away at college, he had been doing it ever since.

"I'm getting along, Ethan. Some days are better than others, but I'm still on this side of the dirt, so I must be doing okay." She laughed at herself.

Ethan smiled and took another drink from his iced tea. He was so parched from the mowing that the glass was soon half empty. "The tea's good." He wanted to say he needed to get going. He also wanted to remind her how much the mowing would cost. She had been getting a little forgetful lately.

She demanded that he fill his glass again and he obliged. "I got my hair fixed this morning. You'll never guess what I heard."

"What's that?"

"Gracie said Olivia is back in town," she said. The big smile returned to her face. Another former favorite pupil of hers. "Isn't that wonderful?"

Ethan covered his frown by bringing the glass to his lips. *Here we go again.* He had spent the past hour mowing Mrs. Sanderson's yard and deliberately trying to pry the thought of Olivia Daniels out of his head. His only response was a single nod.

"I'm so proud of her. She was always such a bright student. And she loved the school plays we used to put on. She could light up a stage with her acting." The gushing praise went on for another minute before she brought Ethan up in her memories. "You two were such an adorable couple."

Ethan looked out the kitchen window. The sigh caused his shoulders to dip slightly. They *had* been an adorable couple. Ever since grade school, everyone said Olivia and Ethan would end up getting married and enjoy a long, blissful life together. But the love affair was over, except in the minds of those who only remembered the days of yesteryear.

"I remember when you two would pass notes to each other in my class. I didn't say anything because I thought it was the cutest thing. Nowadays the kids probably just send messages back and forth on their phones. Have you seen her?"

Ethan didn't want to lie to Mrs. Sanderson. He really just wanted her to write out the check so he could be on his way to the next job. "I saw her heading to the coffee house this morning. Maybe I'll get to talk to her when she gets home." He had no desire to talk to her, but it sounded good to the ears of Mrs. Sanderson.

She reached over and patted Ethan on the hand. "I still have high hopes for you two."

Ethan didn't know whether she meant the two of them together or just hopes for them individually. But it was clear Mrs. Sanderson was not privy to the heartache that Ethan had suffered. He was too good of a man to tell her that he wanted nothing to do with Olivia.

After a third glass of tea and another thirty minutes of chatting, Ethan was finally able to excuse himself from Mrs. Sanderson's kitchen. He left without asking her for payment. It was the third time in a row that she forgot to pay him, but he was too kindhearted to bring it to her attention. She was old, and he felt like he was the only friend she had.

"But I can't keep mowing lawns for free," he told himself as he pulled into his driveway after completion of the two other jobs. The pickup truck with *Stone Landscaping* stenciled on the side rumbled to a stop out front of the only home Ethan Stone ever knew. Born and raised in Huron Cove, he knew every square inch of the land that surrounded the white farmhouse. Of course, the acre of land was immaculate, the grass a lush green and mowed with an artist's touch. Anyone passing by would quickly know their lawn could look the same if only they called Stone Landscaping.

Ethan opened the door of the truck and stepped out. It

had been a long day mowing, weeding, and manicuring the lawns of the handful of clients he had on the schedule. It was satisfying work. He could see the fruits of his labors at the end of the day, and his sweaty shirt told him he had done good work. He just wanted a nice hot shower, a bite to eat, and a night of watching the Tigers on the TV. Maybe if Curt called they might hit the town again. That's what Friday nights were for.

As he walked up the front steps, he couldn't help but look to the north. The Daniels' homestead and their B&B was just across the way. The red Mustang in the driveway told him Olivia was home. For how long, he didn't really want to know.

Opening the front door, the pocket of his shirt vibrated. He wondered if it was Mrs. Sanderson calling to tell him she forgot to pay him and she had the check ready. He grabbed his phone and saw Ann Arbor calling again. "What is it with these people?" One of these days, he was going to answer the call and tell whoever was on the other end to stop calling. And he planned on saying it in such a way that the caller would get the message loud and clear.

He threw his work shirt on top of the washing machine and kicked off his boots. His feet were aching, and his muscles were sore. A shower and something to eat and he'd be ready to do it all again tomorrow. He walked upstairs, took a long hot soak, and threw on a worn Tigers T-shirt. A big bowl of beef stew and a dinner roll filled his stomach. He was starting to feel good. Maybe a night out on the town would be a possibility. He grabbed the remote, turned on the ball game, and dove onto the couch. He rolled forward slightly when the phone buzzed on the coffee table.

"Hey, Curt. What's up?"

"Hey, buddy. I was just calling to see what you're up

to."

"I just got back about a half hour ago. It was a long hot day. Mowed nine yards and cut down two trees for Mr. Curlin."

"Did Mrs. Sanderson talk your ear off?"

Ethan grabbed the remote and muted the TV. "Like always. I got a couple of glasses of iced tea out of it, though."

The silence that followed was noticeable. It wasn't like Curt to be at a loss for words. Ethan would soon know why. "Have you seen Olivia again?"

Ethan gritted his teeth. All day long it had been happening. Olivia this, Olivia that. Why did everyone keep bringing her up? "Come on, man. And no, I haven't seen her again and I don't plan to."

"Is she home?" Curt knew the car would have been out in front of the B&B.

Ethan lied. "I don't know."

"You should probably go over there and say hello. Maybe rekindle the old romance."

"Here we go again. What is wrong with you? I thought you were my friend. Why do you keep bringing her up?"

"Because it's fun."

"Fun? How would you like it if I constantly reminded you about Nicole? Remember Nicole?"

"Hey, that was just a summer fling, Ethan. It's not destiny like you and Olivia." He laughed hard when he said it.

"Whatever." Ethan was one more sarcastic remark away from hanging up on his buddy.

"So, there's no chance of you two reminiscing about the good old days?"

"No. No chance at all."

Ethan had made up his mind a long time ago. There was absolutely nothing that could get Ethan and Olivia back together again. Nothing.

Curt relented for the time being. Maybe tomorrow. Or maybe later on tonight. "You feel like going out? We could head to The Cellar and watch the Tigers on the big screen."

Ethan thought about the offer for a second. Maybe a night out with the guys and a ball game on TV would take his mind off Olivia. His thoughts were interrupted with a knock at his front door.

"Hold on a second, Curt. There's someone at the door."

Ethan walked toward the front door, but his steps slowed. He could see long blonde hair through the sheer curtain over the window. Olivia? His stomach dropped. He really didn't want to deal with her right now. Or any other time for that matter. He opened the door and peeked out. The surprise quickly became evident on his face. It was a twenty-something woman with long blonde hair. But it wasn't Olivia. What's more, neither was the little girl holding a black garbage bag standing next to her.

Ethan covered the phone with his hand. "Can I help you?" he asked through the screen.

The woman took a step forward, the little girl did not. "Are you Ethan Stone?"

Ethan looked at the woman. He then looked down at the girl. Her brown hair was tied in two pigtails that rested on each shoulder. She never took her eyes off the man behind the door. "Yes, I'm Ethan Stone, can I help you?" *Were they lost?* He looked out to see if the pair might have had vehicle trouble.

"Mr. Stone, my name is Ashley White. I'm from the Michigan Department of Child Protective Services office in Ann Arbor. I'm sorry to stop by so late, but I've been trying to contact you for several weeks. I've never gotten an answer and I'm in a bit of a bind here."

Ethan put the phone down to his side. His mind was spinning. Why in the world would CPS be at his house? And why would this woman have been trying to contact him? And who was this little girl? "I'm sorry, Miss . . ."

"White. Ashley White."

"I'm sorry, Miss White. I didn't recognize the number. I don't know too many people in Ann Arbor these days." He stopped to look at her again and then the little girl. "What can I do for you?"

Miss White took a breath. She knew what she had to say would hit the man like a ton of bricks, but she couldn't think of a better way to break the news. "Mr. Stone, this is Emma Lynn Grayson," she said, pointing at the girl. "Your new daughter."

Ethan's mouth fell open. The quick shake of his head made him feel faint. What did she just say? He looked at the little girl again. Her big brown eyes blinked once. Ethan quickly looked back at Miss White. "What is this? Some sort of joke?"

"I'm sorry to spring this on you like this, Mr. Stone. But if we could come in, I'll explain it all in detail. And I can more formally introduce you to your new daughter."

Ethan realized the woman did indeed say the little girl was his daughter. In fact, she said it twice. But he still had no idea what she was talking about. His legs felt like jelly, and he thought he might pass out. He suddenly realized he still had the phone in his hands. He looked at the little girl again before raising the phone to his ear.

"Curt, I'm gonna have to call you back."

CHAPTER 6

"I'm sorry, what?"

Before he asked the question of Miss White, Ethan's first thought was to slam the door in their faces, run to his room, and hide under the bed. He didn't have a daughter! And given that he hadn't even gotten past second base with Olivia, the only woman he had ever been with, it was a pretty good bet that Miss White was sorely mistaken. Somehow Child Protective Services must have gotten him mixed up with a different Ethan Stone. His pulsating heart told him it could happen.

He opened the door, and they walked in. After showing them to the dining room, Ethan sat on the edge of his seat. Thankfully, if he fainted now, he wouldn't have far to fall.

Miss White pulled a chair closer for the little girl. "Again, I'm terribly sorry to bother you at night, Mr. Stone."

Ethan could tell the woman was serious in her apologies. She looked particularly harried. Why? He didn't know and he didn't really care. He was too busy trying to stop his head from spinning.

His new daughter! Was he having some sort of out-of-body experience? Was it a dream? What did Mrs. Sanderson put in that tea?

"Mr. Stone. . . ,"

He raised a hand to stop her. "Please, it's Ethan."

She nodded. "Ethan. Like I said, this is Emma Lynn Grayson," she said, patting the little girl on the knee. The girl now had the garbage bag on her lap. "She's the daughter of Courtney and Shawn Grayson."

Ethan took a breath and drew back slightly. Some of the pieces of the puzzle were starting to at least be turned over. What the puzzle picture would eventually look like was still a mystery, however.

"As you know, your cousins were fatally injured in a car accident five years ago near their home in San Diego."

Ethan nodded that he remembered the sad family story. Two young parents taken too soon and leaving a young daughter behind. "Tragic," he said quietly. He thought he might have met them once at a family reunion. But it was long ago, and definitely before the Graysons had any children.

Miss White looked at Emma. She really didn't want to dredge up the little girl's past in front of her. She then glanced at the TV in the living room. "Ethan, would it be okay if Emma watches some TV while we talk?"

"Of course."

"Emma, would you like to watch TV?"

Ethan watched as the little girl mouthed what sounded like "okay" and nodded her head once. She looked scared, and her eyes were trying to take in everything around her.

"Okay, come on." Miss White put her hand on Emma's back and guided her to the living room. The girl's right hand held tightly to the garbage bag. Ethan just stood and watched. It was still hard to fathom. Miss White said Emma was his daughter!

Once Miss White found a channel to Emma's liking and got her settled on the couch, she returned to the dining room. She and Ethan took a seat with Emma in sight.

"Emma has bounced around the past several years. She was in foster care for six months after the accident. The Graysons' parents were no longer living, and their will provided that Emma's custody would go to her Aunt

Millie and Uncle Charlie in Ypsilanti. It took some time to get it all sorted out, but that's how she found her way to Michigan. She lived with them for three years." Miss White turned her head toward the living room and lowered her voice. She looked back at Ethan. "Unfortunately, Millie and Charlie have passed on, and Emma has been shuttling between foster homes for the past year."

The story struck Ethan in his heart. "Oh, that's too bad."

He was still trying to come to grips why the little girl was in his house. Why hadn't Miss White told him the news over the phone? He cursed himself for not answering her calls. Maybe he could have short-circuited this mess weeks ago. He looked at Emma sitting on the couch. The garbage bag was now next to her, but her little right hand still clutched it tight. He could see her features in the reflective glow of the TV. So little and innocent.

But not his daughter!

Miss White broke the silence of the dining room. "It took me a while to track you down." She stopped to take a breath and deliver the news. "You're the only family she has left, Ethan."

Wait. What? That's what she meant by Emma being his new daughter!

"What are you saying?"

Miss White tried to make her eyes as sympathetic as possible, but they probably came off more as a desperate plea. "Won't you please consider taking her, Ethan? She's a sweetheart of a girl. She's going into the third grade next fall. She's smart as a whip. A little sassy and stubborn at times, but nothing that you can't handle. I'm sure of it."

Ethan cut her off. This woman must be crazy. "Hey, I don't know anything about being a father." He lowered his voice hoping Emma wouldn't hear that he didn't want to be responsible for an eight-year-old girl. "I can't take her in." He stopped to think of a better excuse. "You don't even know me. I could be an axe murderer for all you know."

Miss White smiled. She had Ethan on the defensive. All her hard work might pay off. "Ethan Michael Stone, age twenty five. College degree in landscape management and agronomics. Played baseball at the University of Michigan. Drafted by the Tigers but his dreams of playing in the majors were cut short by rotator cuff problems. Single. Owner and operator of Stone Landscaping, which, I might add, is current on all its taxes and certifications with the great State of Michigan. Attends services at St. Peter's Christian Church."

Ethan's eyes widened. "How do you know all that?"

"It's called a background check, Ethan. I've done a thousand of them. No criminal history. Not even a speeding ticket. I've checked under every rock, and I've even interviewed several people around town who know you." She was convincing. She remembered Ethan's phone call earlier and took a chance at showing off her investigative credentials. "Oh, and your best friend's name is Curt."

Ethan leaned forward, trying to gain back the ground that he was obviously losing. "I can't take care of a little girl. I barely know how to take care of myself."

Miss White looked at her watch. It was getting late, and she had a long drive back to Ann Arbor. She was just about ready to break out the tears to seal the deal. "Look, Ethan. Like I said, you're Emma's only blood relative left. I can take her back to Ann Arbor if you want me to, but let me tell you what that means. It means she'll be shuttled around through the foster-care system for who knows how long. I've got a family in Detroit willing to take her in for the time being. They are my go-to people in an emergency. They're a nice couple, but they've got seven kids under their roof right now. Ages one to fifteen. Emma will be safe, but she'll have to share a bedroom with three other girls for the foreseeable future. Now, maybe I can find her another family, but it will take time." She leaned forward and pointed her finger at him. "So, Mr. Stone. . . . Ethan. . . Do you want me to throw her back into the system to live with strangers or do you want to step up to the plate and help this sweet little daughter of yours have some stability in her life?"

Ethan ran his hands over his face. He couldn't think straight. He couldn't even remember what day it was. His daughter! Why did she keep calling Emma his daughter? Maybe she was a cousin, a long-lost cousin or something, but she wasn't his daughter.

Ethan should have realized Miss White had called Emma his daughter for a reason. Cousins come and go through life, but a daughter is different. Standup guys don't give up on their daughters. She had reeled him in like a Lake Huron walleye.

"Please, Ethan. She's your family."

Ethan looked at the little girl in the living room. He knew his heart wouldn't let him say no. He couldn't abandon her and send her off to strangers. But what was he getting himself into? He thought nothing good could come of this. He turned back to Miss White. "Okay. She can stay for now," he whispered. He then pointed a finger at her. "But only until you find a good family to take her in."

Miss White smiled wide and shook Ethan's hand. "I'll do my best," she said as she got up to leave. She went to say goodbye to Emma, and they both hugged. Miss White then left for Ann Arbor, and Ethan Stone was left in the living room with Emma Lynn Grayson.

His new daughter.

CHAPTER 7

The laughter at the dinner table sounded like old times. Good times when life seemed simpler for the Daniels sisters growing up on the shores of Lake Huron in Huron Cove. Under the watchful eyes of their parents, the three girls swam and kayaked in the lake or played hide-and-seek in the B&B's orchard full of apple and cherry trees. Mr. and Mrs. Daniels had provided their girls with endless amounts of love and support, a Christian education, and a home that they could always come back to. Unfortunately for them, the times when the whole family got together were fewer and farther between. Thanksgiving and Christmas usually brought them back home, so the middle of June was a pleasant surprise for all.

"I can't believe how much you have grown, you little munchkin," Olivia said to her niece, Bella, and giving her a big hug. "It seems like just yesterday you were just yay big." She held her hand about three feet off the floor. "How old are you now?"

"I'm eight."

."Eight years old!" Olivia looked at her older sister Audrey. "Pretty soon she'll be learning to drive."

Audrey patted her only child, who had received the Daniels beauty gene with her long blonde hair, on the shoulder. "I hope not. Bella just finished second grade. I don't know where the time has gone. The year just flew by."

"I wish my year flew by as fast," Beth Daniels said. A

junior at the University of Michigan, she was the only Daniels girl still in school. "I don't think I'm ever going to get out of college. I just want it to be over."

Olivia turned her head and smiled. "You should enjoy it while you can. Pretty soon you'll have to join the real world like the rest of us."

Seated between her grandparents, Bella found the gap in conversation the perfect time for her question. "Aunt Olivia! When are you going to be on TV again? I tell all my friends about you at school!"

Olivia responded with her award-winning smile. "I don't know munchkin." She hated to break her niece's heart. "I don't know. I'll let you know as soon as I find out."

With the passing of Mrs. Daniels's hearty lasagna and warm bread around the table, the family ate to their hearts' content. But Audrey had a question that she wanted to ask since she walked in the door. She put down her fork and cleared her throat.

"Dad, how have you been feeling lately?"

Mr. Daniels's weary eyes told the whole story. He was worn out. "Oh, I'm just fine," he said in a way that said he didn't want his girls to worry. "Your mother is keeping me busy with the B and B. No rest for the weary when the guests are here."

Mrs. Daniels nodded and tried to steer the conversation away from her husband's health. "The Robertsons are here from Phoenix."

"Again?" Beth asked. "What is that three years in a row?"

Mrs. Daniels smiled and handed her husband another slice of bread. "Four years. They have to try to escape the heat of the desert and they say Lake Huron is the perfect place to do it. We love having them."

Mr. Daniels took a drink from his glass of water. "Of course, it's been in the mid-nineties here. But that's a cold snap for them. They're nice people, and they love your mother's blueberry coffee cake."

"I love grandma's blueberry coffee cake too!" Bella interjected, her hand raised to the ceiling.

Audrey was glad to hear that her parents still enjoyed the B&B, but her dad was looking older. There were a few more gray hairs from the last time she saw him. "Do you have anyone helping out?"

Mr. Daniels glanced at his wife across from him and then down at his middle daughter. He still didn't have an answer to Olivia's proposition.

Olivia spoke first. "Bella, why don't you go try on that princess dress I brought you. I bet Grandma and Grandpa would like to see it."

"Can I, Mom?"

Audrey looked at Olivia and got the look from her sister. Olivia wanted an adults-only conversation. "Sure, sweetie, go ahead."

Olivia waited until she heard Bella bound up the steps to the second floor. Then she made the announcement. "I want to take over the B and B."

It was news to both her sisters. "What?" Beth asked. The smile indicated she didn't think her sister was serious. "What are you talking about? How can you run the B and B from California?"

Olivia pointed at her parents. "They're thinking about selling this place!"

Audrey and Beth snapped their attention toward them. "Selling?" Audrey asked. "Our home?"

"We're getting old, girls," Mr. Daniels said.

"That's why I want to come back and run the B and B."

Audrey swung her head back to her sister. "How can

you run this place and continue your acting career?"

Olivia controlled her tears and the morning's waterworks. Her sisters already knew Olivia had been dumped by Gerard, but they still thought she was working on finding her next acting gig. Had she given up her dreams? Did she really want to come back to Huron Cove and run the B&B?

"It's so hard out there in Hollywood." She sighed, and it gave her the same worn-out appearance that her dad had. "I haven't had much work in the last year. A lot of auditions but nothing comes of it. I'm afraid I've peaked."

"So you're just going to give it all up?" Audrey asked. "What about your goal of seeing your name in lights and on the cover of *People* magazine and winning an Academy Award?"

Olivia looked down at the table and tried to come up with the right words. Those had been her dreams since she was a little girl. Her sisters had loved visiting her in Los Angeles, and she knew they got a kick out of seeing her on TV. But those days had come and gone. "I think I need a new star to chase."

"And you think your star is in Huron Cove?" Beth asked.

Olivia nodded. "I truly believe God is calling me back home. Maybe to run the B and B. Maybe for some other reason. But I think it's the right thing to do and the right time to do it."

Once dinner had concluded, the table cleared, and the grandparents and Bella off to bed early, the three Daniels sisters sat cross-legged on Olivia's bed in her old room to talk the night away while doing their nails. Just like old times.

"Do you have any idea how you're going to run this place by yourself?" Audrey asked.

Olivia laughed. Audrey sounded like her parents. "I'm not going to be running it all by myself. Mom and Dad aren't going anywhere. They'll be around to tell me what I'm doing wrong."

"I'll do whatever I can to help," Beth said. She blew gently on her freshly painted nails. "Maybe I can make a project out of it for one of my business classes."

With her parents in the room down the hall, Audrey lowered her voice. "I'm worried about Dad. He doesn't look like he's in good health."

The three sisters had all seen it. Their dad wasn't the strapping young man he used to be. The hair was grayer, and he looked thinner.

"I thought the same thing," Olivia whispered back. "He denies it, but Mom hinted that she sees it too. Did you know they're also thinking about cancelling the Fourth of July fireworks show?"

"What?" Beth said, a bit too loudly. She glanced over at the closed door, hoping she hadn't been so boisterous as to disturb them. "The Fourth of July fireworks are a tradition at the B and B. Guests specifically ask for that week just for the fireworks." She shook her head at the thought. "That would be like cancelling Christmas."

Olivia clutched a pillow to her chest. "I know, but it's a lot of work. That's even more reason for me to come back to help. We can keep the tradition alive, and I know Mom and Dad will be thankful for the show to go on."

Audrey closed the cap on her bottle of light blue polish. Being the oldest, and therefore the wisest, she was more skeptical. "What about taking care of the grounds? Brides want their wedding destinations to be perfect. That means a perfect beach on the lake, a manicured lawn. And have you seen the barn lately? Maybe Dad is going for the rustic look, but to me, it looks a little run down."

"I've noticed that, too," Beth said somberly.

"Olivia, if you're looking to keep the B and B on a firm financial footing, it's going to take a lot of hands-on labor."

Olivia laughed again. "You sound just like Dad. Next thing you'll want to do is check my hands to see if they've ever had any dirt on them." She looked down at her pink nails but said no more. Maybe Audrey and her dad were right. Maybe she didn't have what it took.

Audrey could see the workings of her sister's mind. She had no trouble giving Olivia her honest answers, but that didn't mean she was going to douse whatever spark Olivia had for her life. She offered the only thing she could think of. "Why don't you hire Ethan to help?"

Olivia looked out the window. She could see Ethan's house in the distance. They had school-kid crushes on each other since kindergarten. Over the years as their love blossomed, they would use flashlights to blink messages to one another. Three short bursts meant "I love you." Every night during high school ended with those flashes. But it had been a long time since then, and the light had slowly faded away. She told Gerard about it once, but he belittled it as something juvenile, certainly nothing for cultured romantics. Still looking out the window, she said, "Dad said the same thing."

She didn't know whether she wanted to ask Ethan for help or even if she could. One thing she did know—she wondered what he was doing in his house across the way.

CHAPTER 8

Ethan and Emma sat for what seemed like a lifetime in the living room in front of the TV. Ethan had muted it, and that made the silence even more deafening if that was possible. Neither of them had said anything. Neither of them even realized the Tigers were up by five runs over the Yankees in the bottom of the seventh. Right now, neither of them cared. Both looked at each other trying to figure out what was going on.

His daughter!

Ethan kept telling himself that it was just temporary. She wasn't really his daughter. He was just going to take care of her until Miss White could find a nice couple to take her in and off his hands. Hopefully it would just be a day or two. Maybe a few more given the weekend. Someday they'd both probably laugh about it at a family reunion.

"So, Ella, how old are you?"

She looked at him with big brown eyes like those little girls in the *Despicable Me* movies. She licked her lips and spoke clearly. "My name is Emma. Emma Lynn Grayson. And I'm eight years old."

Ethan nodded and silently chided himself. He couldn't even get his own daughter's name right! Further proof he wasn't up to the task. "So, you go by Emma?"

"Yes."

He was at a loss for words. He had half expected to

spend the evening with Curt and his buddies discussing the finer points of the Tigers-Yankees game—batting averages, home runs, runs batted in. Maybe they would even debate the infield-fly rule and three-inning saves. But here he sat in his living room with an eight-year-old girl he didn't even know. Weren't there laws against such things?

After more awkward staring, Ethan finally thought of something to ask. "Are you hungry or thirsty? I could get you something to eat or drink."

Emma shook her head. "No, I'm fine, thank you."

He wondered who he could call. His parents were deceased, and he had no siblings. He could call Curt, but his friend would probably bust out laughing at the story or think Ethan was putting him on with a made-up reason for not wanting to go out. Somehow his mind reached into the deep dark crevasses and brought up the name Olivia Daniels. She was home. A woman would know what to do. Should he call her?

No. No way. This was his problem. Correction—temporary problem. He could deal with it.

Ethan noticed Emma wore khaki shorts with a plain pink T-shirt. Her shoes were pink with white laces. "Do you want me to throw away your garbage?"

Emma scrunched her eyebrows and then glanced down at the bag next to her. She shook her head. "This is my stuff."

"Your stuff?"

"My clothes. My belongings."

Ethan looked closer at the bag and his stomach dropped. There didn't seem to be much in it. "That's all you've got?"

"Yes." Bouncing around homes didn't lead to the accumulation of many possessions. Emma used both hands to undo the end of the bag. "It's mostly clothes, my book, my toothbrush, and my hair brush." She reached inside and pulled out a stuffed Teddy bear. "And Wilfred."

Ethan's laughter helped lessen the tension in the room as he looked at the brown furry bear with a red bandana wrapped around his neck. "Wilfred? That's his name?"

Emma smiled because Ethan found it so funny. "Yes. Wilfred E. Goodbear."

Ethan stood up and then knelt down in front of Emma. He grabbed hold of the bear after she held it out for him to see. "Wilfred E. Goodbear. What's the 'E' stand for?"

"Eugene."

Ethan laughed again. "Eugene!" He thought this girl had a sense of humor. He liked that. "What else you got in there?"

Emma reached into the bag, pulled out a book, and handed it to Ethan.

"*Anne of Green Gables*. Lucy Maud Montgomery," he said, reading the cover. He noticed the book was well-worn. "Have you read it?"

"Yes. Several times. It's my favorite book." She looked at her bag again. "My only book."

Ethan caught the sad tone in Emma's voice. He wondered what she had been through in her short life. How many tears had she shed at her predicament? The loss of her parents. The moving around. The death of her Aunt Millie and Uncle Charlie. More moving around. Now she was here, thrust into yet another world of unknowns. He wanted to give her a hug. It was right then that Ethan told himself he was going to make her life as comfortable as possible.

At least until Miss White found a nice husband and wife to take care of her.

She opened her bag a little more. "Everything else is clothes."

Ethan craned his neck to peer inside. There looked to be a white dress, a pair of jeans, some socks, shorts, and some T-shirts.

Emma pulled one item out. "This is my nightshirt."

Ethan took it and held it up. The shirt was large, much too big for her—thus the reason for it being a nightshirt. He turned it around and read the writing on the front. "*I'm not tipsy, I'm from Ypsi.*" Overlaid on an outline of Michigan, a picture of a martini glass with two olives in it hovered over the location of Ypsilanti just west of Detroit. He looked at Emma and raised an eyebrow.

She was smart enough to know what he was thinking. "It was Aunt Millie's. She won it at bingo. She never wore it so she said I could have it. She just said I couldn't wear it out in public."

Ethan folded up the shirt and handed it back to her. "Probably a pretty good idea." He took a seat on the couch, the garbage bag and Wilfred in between him and Emma. "Do you miss Aunt Millie and Uncle Charlie?"

"Yeah. Uncle Charlie died before I got to know him very well, but I loved being around Aunt Millie. We read the Bible together and then we cooked in the kitchen. We made lots of cookies and took them to people who were shut-in. And then at night we'd watch *Jeopardy!* She was really good at trivia."

Ethan and Emma talked for another hour before he finally looked at his watch. It was late, and both of them had had a long day in more ways than one. He rummaged through the hall closet and found a clean towel she could use if she needed it. He put some fresh sheets on the bed in the spare room and showed her where the bathroom was down the hall.

With her *I'm not tipsy, I'm from Ypsi* nightshirt on and her teeth brushed, Ethan tucked her into bed. He couldn't believe he was doing this. This was something fathers do. He wasn't a father. He was Ethan Stone—Huron Cove's most eligible bachelor. "I'm just down the hall if you need anything."

She clutched Wilfred tighter. "Okay. Thank you, Mr. Stone."

He thought about telling her to call him Ethan, but he didn't. He was too exhausted. "Do you want me to leave the hallway light on for you."

"Yes, sir, that would be nice. Thank you."

"Okay." He walked to the door and switched off the light. "Good night, Emma."

"Good night."

Ethan left her bedroom door ajar and turned on the hallway light. He went to his bedroom, shut his door, and changed his clothes. He collapsed into bed and stared at the ceiling. He woke this morning living an uninhibited lifestyle—free to do whatever he wanted, whenever he wanted. Now he had to figure out a way to get rid of this new anchor weighing him down.

"What in the world am I going to do now?"

* * *

Back in her room, Emma's eyes had yet to close, and her ears strained to listen for every sound emitted by her new surroundings. The house was old, and the creaky floorboards would tell her whether anyone was coming. They might also tell someone whether she was going. She couldn't run away, and she had no desire to do so. She wasn't sure exactly where Huron Cove was on the map, just that it was a good distance north of Ann Arbor on the shores of Lake Huron. At least she had her trusty Wilfred by her side. Thinking Ethan may be in bed for the rest of the night, she slipped out from under the covers and got out of bed. She knelt down beside it and folded her hands.

"Dear Lord," she whispered. She looked to make sure no one was outside her door. "Thank you for bringing me into this new home. Mr. Stone seems like a really nice guy. I know he doesn't want me, Lord, but mightn't you help change his mind. He is family after all. I also know Miss White says she wants to find a husband and a wife to take me in, but maybe you could find Mr. Stone a nice wife. He is handsome, and I haven't seen any sign of him being attached. Just some thoughts. If there's anything I can do to help, just let me know. Please say hello to Mommy and Daddy and Aunt Millie and Uncle Charlie in heaven. Amen."

CHAPTER 9

The sun peeking over the horizon was something Olivia would never forget about growing up in Huron Cove. How blessed she had been to have lived on the shores of Lake Huron and to have the opportunity to watch the sun rise over the water to start the day. Sure, the sunsets in Los Angeles were beautiful—when the smog didn't spoil the view—but the quiet serenity of a Michigan sunrise meant she was home.

"Well, look who's up," her dad said as he walked into the kitchen. "I thought I smelled the coffee brewing." He walked over and gave Olivia a kiss on the forehead. "You're up bright and early considering all that late-night laughing I heard from your room last evening."

Olivia handed him a fresh mug of piping hot coffee. "Oh, Dad, I'm sorry. Did we keep you up?"

Mr. Daniels took a drink and smiled. "Sweetie, hearing you and your sisters laughing is music to my ears. I miss it. Your mom misses it, too. We're glad to have you girls back home. At least for a while." He finished his cup and looked out the window. "Another beautiful sunrise. Pure Michigan if you ask me." He then looked at Olivia. "You ready to get after it?"

Olivia took a deep breath and smiled. "Ready as I'll ever be."

"Okay, then. Let's go."

Father and daughter headed out into the Huron Cove morning and took in their first breaths of the outdoors.

"Bet you don't get this in California?"

"Definitely not in the city. Maybe if you head inland to one of the lakes, but it's so crowded with people trying to get away that it's not worth going there."

Her father wore his usual blue jeans and light red flannel. He went with the short sleeves, knowing it was going to be another warm one. The boots were well worn with spots of mud caked on them. He didn't say anything about his daughter's attire. Her boots were black leather lace-ups by Gucci, and they looked like they were fresh out of the box. The jeans were Dolce & Gabbana, and the white button-down shirt was Ralph Lauren. Olivia looked like she had just stepped out from in front of the lens of a fashion photographer. Her father smiled. He hoped she didn't pay a lot for her clothes because, by the end of the day, she might not want to wear them again.

Olivia, however, felt invigorated. She was ready to dive right in to her new calling in life. She was going to make sure the Huron Cove B&B was the best vacation and wedding destination in the world. She even hoped her dad would let her drive the tractor! She knew how to drive a car. How hard could it be?

"All right, first thing I like to do every morning is walk the beach. For one thing, it's good for the soul. And two, I want to make sure there's nothing fouling up the scenery. Every once in a while I'll find a dead bird or something. Guests don't want to have to deal with dead animals." He pointed toward the north. "I go all the way to the lighthouse."

"It's so pretty and peaceful out here, Dad. Just like I always remembered. I haven't realized how much I missed it."

Mr. Daniels hit the beach with his daughter in tow. He noticed she looked at the sand starting to collect on her fancy boots. He looked away to smile. "I do enjoy the walks in the morning. It gets the blood pumping and reminds me how thankful I am that God provided us with such a beautiful spot on this earth."

The pair made it to the lighthouse without finding any dead fowl or anything amiss. Soon the area would be teeming with tourists as they took pictures of one of Michigan's famous landmarks. While the Daniels didn't own the white brick lighthouse with the red barber-pole stripe, they had acted as overseers of it and the red-brick keeper's house and museum for over two decades. Thus, they had an eye for making sure the area was in good shape. Olivia knew the B&B's wedding couples would want a view of the lighthouse, and she would make sure to give them the best shot possible.

Standing at the base, Olivia looked up to the glass-enclosed lantern room at the top. "Do you and Mom remember teaching us girls how to count by climbing up the lighthouse steps?"

Mr. Daniels smiled. "I remember that. It was a good teaching tool. At least up to number seventy-eight." He unlocked the door. "Let's go up."

Olivia followed right behind and up the spiral staircase. By halfway, she could tell her dad was slowing. "You want to take a break and rest a minute?"

Mr. Daniels looked down behind him. "We're almost there."

Once at the top, Olivia soaked in the gorgeous views—Lake Huron as far as the eye could see to the east and her family's land below to the west. "It's beautiful." She told herself there was no way they were going to sell the B&B. This was more than enough reason to want to come back home.

Mr. Daniels read her mind. He wanted to bring her up

there for a reason. He pointed to the beach and then the B&B cottages, the barn, and the orchard. "There's a lot to take care of, Olivia."

Olivia understood her father's tone. "I know, Dad. But this is what I want to do." She spread her arms wide. "This is what I want to continue."

Mr. Daniels put an arm around her. Maybe she was stubborn enough to make it work. They headed back down. "Once I check the grounds of the lighthouse, I head back to the cottages. Breakfast for the guests is usually eight o'clock unless someone wants an early or late start. Your mom drives the food down in the golf cart about ten minutes till."

"The grass looks nice," Olivia said, as she looked out over the misty dew covering the green carpet around the cottages.

Her dad nodded but frowned. "The mower's been acting up. I think it might need a new oil filter."

"Okay." She wondered if she should start taking notes.

"I'll show you how to change the oil later. I try to mow the grass a couple of times a week. But only if the guests aren't in their cottages. We don't want to disturb them if they're here for some rest and relaxation."

"That sounds appropriate."

Her father stopped her once they reached the gazebo. "Here, help me clear out this dead debris from the rose bushes."

After watching her father's hands dive right in to clear away the dead leaves, she did the same. "Ow!" she said, pulling her right hand back. She winced and shook it.

"Did you get a thorn in you?"

Olivia shook her hand some more and then looked down at her fingers. "No, I just broke a nail."

Her father grabbed her hand and suppressed his laugh.

City girl. The once beautiful pink nail looked like it had been bitten by a shark. "Yeah, that'll happen." With that attempt at consoling her done, he turned and went back to picking off the white roses that were looking a bit ragged. He wondered if she would make it until noon. Maybe now was the time to hint she should stick to the event planning side of things. "Have you given any more thought to asking Ethan if he's interested in some extra work?"

Olivia didn't respond immediately. She looked down at her boots, which had gone from dirty to muddy within a hundred yards. Then she looked at her deformed nail. She wondered what her hands would look like once her dad had her changing the oil in the mower. *Oh boy.* The doubts about whether she could pull this off were starting to creep in. Actually, they weren't creeping, they were charging at her like raging bulls.

She had thought a lot about Ethan last night after her sisters had gone to bed. She almost called him. She had noticed all the lights in his house were on, which was odd. Maybe he was having people over. Anyway, she went over every scenario in her mind. How she would approach him. What she would say. She knew full well he'd balk at even talking to her, let alone agreeing to work for her. She didn't know what to do.

"I thought maybe I could put an ad in the paper." She looked over at her dad for a response. "You know, 'gardener wanted.'"

Her dad didn't stop to answer. He walked up the gazebo steps and fluffed up the pillows on the swing. "Where do you think you're going to find a gardener, sweetie? And is that all you think you'd need?" He grabbed a rag out of his back pocket and wiped down the railings. "I bet it'd take two *gardeners* to do all it takes to keep this place humming." He took a moment to take a breath. "Do you want me to call Ethan and talk to him. I'll do it. Maybe it would make it easier on him." He patted Olivia on the shoulder with his dirty glove. "And maybe it would be easier on you."

Olivia turned her eyes toward Ethan's house, the sun's rays shining off the white siding. She reminded herself that she was doing this not only for her, but for her parents and the B&B. She could do this.

"No, I'll talk to him, Dad. I need to make amends with Ethan one of these days. Maybe I'll have a breakthrough with him once he knows the B and B is involved."

"That's my girl," her dad said, patting her on the back. Her blouse sure wouldn't be making it past noon. He pointed off to their house. "Look, there's your mom with breakfast. I think the Robinsons must be getting an early start this morning. They might be heading up to Mackinac. You want to join us?"

Olivia smiled at her dad and gave him a hug. It had been an eye-opening morning for her. She had forgotten all the work that went into the B&B. "No, I better go find Ethan. I've got a lot of work to do."

CHAPTER 10

Ethan woke to bright sunshine peeking through the curtains. He looked at his watch and realized it was almost seven o'clock. He had slept surprisingly well. It probably had something to do with the mental and physical exhaustion that he had to endure yesterday. Seeing Olivia in the morning and then a full day's work. And then! The arrival of Emma Lynn Grayson.

He shook the cobwebs and wondered if he had dreamt it all. What a wild dream it would be if that were the case. Maybe if he tiptoed out of his bedroom, he'd walk down the hall and find the spare room empty. Nothing amiss. It had all been a figment of his wild imagination. Then his life would go back to the normal carefree days he was used to.

He listened for any sounds of life down the hall. Nothing but silence. He smiled. He almost laughed out loud. That's what it had to be. It had to have been a dream. He let out a relaxing breath. Wait until Curt and Arlene hear about this over coffee. He threw off the covers and yawned. He stopped to think what was on his agenda today. Nothing much. Pick up some supplies and buy some groceries. He'd probably go out with Curt and live it up tonight.

He got out of bed and stretched his arms high above his head. "Man, I'm hungry. I can't even remember what I had for dinner last night."

He opened the door to his bedroom and laughed at

himself again. Once he tells people his silly dream, they're going to wonder what he was drinking before he went to bed. But his forward progress stopped immediately. The door to the spare bedroom was open. He always kept it closed. Had he left it open? Had he been sleepwalking last night and gone into the room? Surely it was just a dream. Wasn't it?

He inched forward. *No, no, no. It can't be true.* He prayed it was a dream. *Oh please, let it be a dream.* He didn't have a daughter. He was an unattached bachelor living a carefree existence—not a father to an eight-year-old girl. He heard nothing. What's behind door number one? He craned his head around the doorjamb and then his shoulders slumped.

"Good morning, Mr. Stone."

His first instinct was to run away, as if he saw a mouse or a monster or a burglar or something. Instead, he showed himself in the doorway and put his hands on his hips. She was wearing a dark pair of shorts and a pink tank top with cartoon Minions down the front. It was not what she had on yesterday, so she must have dug it out of her garbage bag. The comforter on the bed had been pulled back so tight it would impress a four-star general. Wilfred E. Goodbear sat up straight against the headboard. She stood next to the bed, her hands clasped in front of her, the picture of sweetness.

But she was real. Flesh and blood real. She wasn't part of some weird dream. She was standing right there next to the bed and looking at him.

He nodded at her and started to say something. He stopped himself to make sure to get her name right this time. "Good morning, Emma. How did you sleep?"

"Very well, thank you, Mr. Stone."

"That's good." Ethan suddenly remembered he had yet

to take a shower. Maybe that would help him figure out what to do. First things first, though. "Emma, you don't have to call me Mr. Stone. You can call me Ethan."

Emma smiled sweetly. "Okay, thank you."

"I'm going to take a shower, and then I'll fix us some breakfast. Feel free to watch TV if you want."

Ethan let the warm water of the shower wash over him. His mind raced with a thousand thoughts swirling through his head. What had he gotten himself into? Why hadn't he just told Miss White to take Emma back to Ann Arbor? What was he going to do now? What would people say? He needed to talk to somebody. He knew that much. "Maybe Arlene will know what to do."

Once dressed and down the stairs, he found Emma in the picture window seat reading *Anne of Green Gables*. The sunlight surrounded her with a celestial glow. When she saw him, she closed her book and hopped to her feet. She stood ramrod straight, chin up with a ready smile. A four star would have been ready to fire off a return salute.

"At ease, Emma. You don't have to stand at attention every time I walk into a room."

"Okay, thank you, Mr. Sto . . ., I mean, Mr. Ethan."

He shook his head at her politeness. At least she was polite. She could have been one of those rude snot-nosed brats that he had seen at restaurants, but, so far at least, she was a well-mannered young girl. "Let's see what we have for breakfast."

Emma followed him into the kitchen and stood next to him when he opened the fridge.

Ethan grunted. "Not much in here. I was going to go to the store today to pick up a few things." He grabbed what was left in the milk jug, twisted off the cap, brought the opening to his nose, and then quickly took it away. "Augh. I think that's gone bad." He offered to let her take a whiff, but she frowned and made a face. She'd take his word for it. He replaced the cap and put the jug back on the shelf. "I'll have to put milk down on the list." There were a couple of other jars and some containers, but nothing appropriate for breakfast. "Looks like we'll have to pick something up to eat when we go into town." He shut the door and looked her over. "You ready to go?"

"Yes, sir."

Ethan frowned some more. There she goes again with the formalities. She was too sweet looking for him to lecture her. "Okay, let's go."

The pair didn't make it far before Ethan stopped cold as he reached for the door handle. Through the curtains he saw the beautiful blonde hair of Olivia Daniels as she walked across the lawn toward his house.

"Oh great," he whispered to himself. He didn't want to deal with her right now. He looked down at Emma standing next to him and realized he *really* didn't want to deal with Olivia right now. "Quick, hide."

"What? I thought we were going into town."

Ethan stammered as best he could. "Um . . . Just give me a minute to get rid of this lady and then we'll go."

Emma didn't know what to make of it or Ethan's nervousness. She backed away into the living room so whoever was coming wouldn't see her.

Ethan steeled himself for what was to come. He had thought he could make it through the weekend without talking to the woman who crushed his heart just a couple of years ago. Then she'd fly back to La-La Land and be out of his life again. Maybe she was coming to rip off the bandage once more by telling him she was getting married. He took a deep breath and told himself to keep it short. He opened the door when Olivia stepped onto the front porch. He let her speak first.

Olivia stopped three feet short of the door, slightly weary of treading on Ethan's home turf like she had so many times before. She hoped he would hear her out. "Hi, Ethan."

Ethan didn't fully open the door. He stood between it and the jamb, his body language indicating he expected her to go no further. An invitation to enter would not be in the cards. "Hi."

"Can we talk?" She gestured her hand toward him and back to her a couple of times.

Ethan sighed and couldn't keep from offering a quick shake of his head. He was slightly amused at her muddy boots and dirty jeans. Who would have thought Olivia Daniels would ever be seen out in public with such sartorial imperfections.

"Olivia, now's not a good time."

* * *

Olivia brushed a strand of hair out of her face. She could see the hurt in his eyes. But there was something else. She noticed how rigid he appeared. She tried to peer behind him. "Please, Ethan. I really need to talk to you. It's not about us." She knew she was treading on shaky ground with even mentioning "us." "It's about the B and B. I'm taking over the operations from my parents because my dad isn't doing great. He can't keep doing everything by himself. I was wondering if you'd be willing to take on a new project."

He grimaced. "I'm not sure that's a good idea, Olivia, given the way things have been in the past."

"It's strictly an employment opportunity, Ethan. We'll pay you well, of course."

"I still don't know. Maybe we could talk some other time." He looked at his watch to hurry her along. "I need to get going."

Olivia glanced through the curtained side windows. It was then that it struck her.

Ethan Stone had a woman in there! That's why he was being so standoffish. She stepped back. She couldn't believe it. Sure, she couldn't expect Ethan to remain alone for the rest of his life, but it was so unlike him to have a woman over for a one-night stand. Or maybe the woman was living with him. Perhaps he wasn't the guy he used to be.

Could it be that Olivia had changed him for the worse?

"I'm sorry, Ethan. I didn't know." She turned around, wanting to run back home. "I'll call you sometime when it's more convenient."

* * *

Ethan relaxed a bit now that disaster had been averted. "Okay, thank you. Maybe some other time." He shut the door and watched her leave, thankful that he didn't have to talk to Olivia about their past or explain why he had an eight-year-old girl hiding in his living room.

CHAPTER 11

Once Olivia was nowhere to be seen and the coast was clear, Ethan hustled to the truck and hopped into the cab as Emma scampered into the seat next to him. He didn't even have to tell her to fasten her seatbelt. She clicked it into place and turned her eyes out the window.

Ethan turned the key and the Ford pickup rumbled to life. He didn't say a word to Emma, but his eyes never strayed from Olivia's place.

"Who was that woman?"

Ethan released the brake and grabbed the shifter. He kept his eyes to the north. He hadn't realized Emma had seen Olivia. "Just some woman."

Emma looked over at Ethan and noticed a trickle of sweat running down the side of his face. "I saw her when I was peeking around the curtain in the living room. Is she a friend of yours?"

Ethan had purposefully said "some woman" because he didn't want to say she was an "old friend." Olivia was a part of his past, and he wanted her to stay that way. "I just know her."

"She's beautiful. It's almost like I've seen her before."

Ethan grunted. Hadn't everybody? Once they reached the end of the lane and turned onto the blacktop, he relaxed a bit. He got rid of one problem by giving Olivia the cold shoulder, but now. What to do with the brown-eyed girl sitting next to him?

"It's very pretty here," Emma said to him. "I didn't get to see much of it last night when we were driving up here because of the late hour."

"Most people say it's pretty. That's why we get a lot of tourists in Huron Cove."

"I like the lighthouse." She pointed to Huron Cove's famous landmark. "That's pretty cool. Did you know Michigan has more lighthouses than any other state?"

"Is that so?"

"Yep. There are over a hundred of them."

"How'd you get so smart?"

"I like school." She didn't turn her head toward him. She was too busy trying to take in all of the passing scenery. "And Aunt Millie liked to tell me all about Michigan. She loved living here. Said God blessed the State of Michigan beyond measure." She then turned her head toward Ethan. "I'm not sure exactly what 'beyond measure' means but I think it means a lot."

Ethan flicked the turn signal and made a right at the stop sign. Down another quarter of a mile, he eased the truck into a parking spot out front of The Coffee Cove and jammed the shifter into park. Before he could tell Emma to wait in the truck, she had unbuckled and thrown open the door.

"Oh, boy," Ethan muttered.

She used both hands and gave an eight-year-old's grunt to swing the heavy Ford door shut. She then hopped onto the sidewalk and surveyed in every direction. "This is a nice little town."

Ethan said nothing. He was mentally preparing himself for whatever would confront him on the other side of The Coffee Cove's glass door. He was the hot hunk of Huron Cove, on the radar screens of any number of older women trying to fix him up with their available daughter, niece, or neighbor. Now? He was going to walk in with an eight-year-old girl trailing him.

"Good morning, Ethan."

Ethan strode forward, his eyes looking for Curt and expecting him to start asking a boatload of questions he didn't have answers to. "Good morning, Arlene."

"I haven't seen your partner-in-crime this morning." She reached for a cup and then a pot of coffee. "Is he still sleeping it off or has he even called it a night yet?"

Ethan grabbed his cup, took a sip, and closed his eyes. "Ah, just what I needed." After a few seconds, he opened his eyes and looked at Arlene. "I actually didn't go out with Curt last night so I'm not sure where he is."

Arlene gave him back his change. "Taking my advice, are you?"

Ethan smiled. "Something like that."

When Ethan took another sip, Arlene's attention went to the little girl behind him and to the side. She hadn't seen Emma come in behind Ethan, and the girl didn't look familiar. "Can I help you, little darlin'?"

Ethan snapped out of his caffeine-induced buzz and realized Arlene wasn't talking to him. He turned to see Emma looking up at him. *Guess it's time to do some explaining.* He bent down toward her and pointed at the glass case. "Would you like a chocolate muffin?"

"Yes, thank you."

He whispered some more. "Why don't you go snag that table over there for us, okay? Do you want some chocolate milk, too?"

"Sure, thank you."

Once Emma was out of earshot, Ethan turned back to Arlene, whose eyes were as big as her famous giant muffins.

"Uh, Ethan. You want to fill me in on what's going on

here?"

He caught Arlene's surprised look and then pointed over at Emma. Then it was back to Arlene. "Oh, no. It's not what it looks like." He stammered for something coherent and leaned toward the counter. "She's a cousin of mine or something. I don't really know. I'm just watching her for a day or two until some people down in Ann Arbor figure out what they're doing. Can I get two chocolate muffins and a chocolate milk?"

Arlene grabbed a tray. She swiped a tissue out of the box and reached down into the case for two chocolate muffins. "I was beginning to wonder. I thought maybe there might have been a part of your life that I didn't know about." She turned around, opened up the mini-fridge, and pulled out a carton of chocolate milk. "How old is she?"

Ethan turned his eyes toward Emma. She was standing next to the wall looking at a giant roadmap of Michigan. She traced her finger north from Ypsilanti in her attempt to find Huron Cove. She was too short to make it all the way. Even on her tiptoes, she only made it to Bay City. "She's eight," Ethan said. "Very polite little thing."

"Just be thankful she's not a teenager. They're a handful. She sure is a cutie, though." Arlene realized who she was talking to. "What are you *two* going to do today?"

Ethan leaned on the counter closer to her. "To be truthful, Arlene, I'm not sure what to do. I don't know how long I'll have her. Any advice?"

"Well, I hope you're not going to take her to Curt's and teach her any of your guys' bad habits." She cocked her head and gave him a look that said she would have something to say about that.

Ethan shook his head. He wasn't that bad of an adult male. "Don't worry. We'll be fine."

She put a couple of napkins on Ethan's tray. "Why

don't you ask Olivia for help?"

Ethan's eyes narrowed. Was Curt feeding questions into Arlene's ear via radio earpiece? It sounded like something Curt would ask. Here they were mentioning Olivia again.

"Olivia used to babysit my girls when she was in high school. Why don't you give her a call."

Ethan thanked her for the food but said nothing more. He grabbed his tray and walked to the table. He told himself he didn't need any help from Olivia. He and Emma would eat some breakfast, and maybe then he'd figure out what to do.

"We're a lot farther north than I thought," Emma said, glancing back up at the map. "Does it get really cold up here in the winter?"

Ethan placed a muffin on a napkin and slid it over. "It's not too bad. Just your typical cold days and nights."

Before he finished his response, Emma was already on her second bite of muffin. She took big bites, like she was afraid if she didn't someone would take it from her before she finished. "These are good. Aunt Millie used to make good blueberry muffins. She taught me how to bake. I can cook if you want me to." She took a swig of milk to wash down another mouthful. "This is a nice place. It smells like fresh coffee. Aunt Millie always liked her coffee in the morning. She called it a cup of joe, but I don't why. I like the hardwood floors, too. It feels like an old-country store in here. I bet it's nice and warm when the fireplace is going during the winter."

Ethan ate in silence, content to look at the lovely little creature who had somehow found her way into his life last evening. He had always wanted kids. And he especially wanted a daughter—one he could spoil and take care of. He thought he would have a family by now, but Olivia crushed those dreams. And now he didn't know whether he could ever open his heart to love again.

"What are we going to do today?"

"I," Ethan said before stopping. He wasn't sure why he stopped, but he did. "I mean we have to stop at the hardware store and then get some groceries."

The pair finished their breakfast, and Ethan picked up a sharpened blade for his lawn mower at the hardware store. Then it was to the Food Mart to pick up something to fill the fridge.

Ethan wasn't used to shopping on a Saturday morning. Usually it was late at night when he remembered he needed a gallon of milk or had to pick up some chips to take to Curt's. As he pushed the shopping cart through the aisles with Emma at his side, he caught the stares of several women. He wasn't sure if they liked a man with a daughter or were disappointed of seeing such a handsome man with one.

He grabbed all the staples—bread, milk, bananas—then he threw in some chips and pop and everything else a man needed. He didn't ask Emma what she wanted.

"Your total is thirty-five dollars and sixty-three cents," the cashier said.

Ethan looked in his wallet and saw he only had a twenty. He pulled out his plastic and gave it a swipe. The machine didn't beep, it buzzed. Beeping was good, buzzing was not.

"Try it again," the cashier said.

Ethan swiped the card through the machine but the dreaded buzzing reared its ugly head. The cashier turned the machine and read the code.

"I'm sorry, sir. Your card's been declined."

Ethan could feel the sweat pooling at the top of his

forehead. Emma looked up at him with concerned eyes, and he could feel the stares of the woman waiting impatiently in line behind him.

"I thought I paid my bill last month." He tried to laugh to lighten the mood but it didn't work. Another swipe would be a wasted effort. He looked at the conveyor of food and had to make a decision—either apologize to the cashier and walk out in shame or try to cut back on what he had.

He went with the latter. "Why don't you take off the chips and the twelve pack and the beef jerky." He added a few more items and prayed the new total would be enough.

The cashier hoped so too because she was going to have to endure the wrath of those in line behind him, which was now three deep, when Ethan and Emma left. "Twenty dollars and two cents."

Ethan's shoulders slumped slightly as he pulled out the twenty.

The cashier smiled and grabbed two coins from the Give-A-Penny-Take-A-Penny tray. "That'll do it. Have a nice day."

Emma said nothing as they got back into the truck with two bags of groceries. She knew better than to talk now.

Ethan, embarrassed beyond belief, tried to remember what the problem was. Did he forget to pay his bill? He knew he was having trouble staying afloat, but was it that bad? He glanced over at Emma, who was looking out the window and watching her new world pass her by. Another mouth to feed. He was responsible for her now, but he could barely make ends meet.

He thought it was going to take a miracle to get out of this mess.

CHAPTER 12

Olivia was sitting with her head in her hand at the kitchen table when her sisters returned from the store with bags full of groceries.

"What's wrong, Olivia?" Beth asked.

Audrey left the groceries on the counter and went to her sister. "Is everything okay?"

Olivia looked at both of her sisters. "I'm not sure I know the full extent of what I'm getting myself into with the B and B."

The youthful Beth laughed. "That's not a total surprise, Olivia. Dad told us about your little sojourn in the mud."

The more serious Audrey did her best to suppress a smile but added a little jab. "And the broken nail."

Olivia sighed and put her head back in her hand. She offered a slight chuckle because she didn't know what else to do. The fingernail had been fixed, the designer clothes changed. She was again the picture of perfection. But maybe she wasn't cut out for the manual labor side of the B&B. "It's a lot more work than I remembered. Mom and I haven't even gotten to the cooking and planning part yet. If I don't find some help on the outdoor labor part of the business, it's not going to be pretty."

Once the groceries were put away, Beth grabbed three glasses, a fresh pitcher of iced tea, and joined her two sisters at the table. "Weren't you going to ask Ethan for help?"

Olivia sat back in her chair and shook her head. "I

went over there this morning and mentioned it."

Beth filled three glasses and passed one to Audrey and then Olivia. "What did he say?"

Audrey wouldn't let Olivia answer. "Is he still mad at you for dumping him?"

Olivia was slightly taken aback at Audrey's forthrightness, but she was right.

"Sometimes when you break off an engagement with a guy and jet off with another man, it can cause hard feelings."

Olivia's eyes widened as she looked at Audrey. Shouldn't her sister be trying to comfort her? "I didn't break off the engagement. I just said no."

"Still. It's something that's been known to leave a bad taste in a man's mouth."

Beth took a drink and then broke up her sisters' conversation. "So he said he wouldn't take the job?"

Olivia shook her head. "He didn't really give me an answer." She stopped before dropping the bombshell. "I think he had a woman in there."

Beth just about gagged on her tea. "A woman!"

Olivia nodded. "I know. It's so unlike Ethan. He was always such a straight arrow."

Beth agreed. "I never thought Ethan would fool around like that. He has always been a God-fearing man ever since I've known him. Shacking up with a woman before marriage is totally out of character for him."

Audrey continued with her dour news. "Mom says he stopped coming to church after you left. He said he didn't feel up to it."

Olivia's shoulders sagged. Had she broken his heart and driven him away from God?

"Are you sure he was with a woman?" Beth asked. "I can't believe it."

Olivia shrugged. "I can't say for sure, but he wouldn't let me inside. I saw the curtains move when I was on the front porch talking to him."

Audrey shook her head at what she was hearing. "Maybe you turned him into a cad."

Olivia wondered if maybe she had. Did she ruin his life forever? Did she turn him into some player who would go from woman to woman and never find everlasting love?

Beth got up from the table and put the pitcher of iced tea back in the fridge. "What are you going to do?"

"I guess I'll have to ask him again. If he's found someone, it might make it easier for both of us to focus on the business. Whatever the case, I need him to help run the B and B. Without him, I'm afraid that this place won't be what the guests expect of us. And I know how much that will upset Mom and Dad. They can't bear to see this place anything other than immaculate." She rubbed her face with both hands. "And then there's the fireworks."

Audrey nodded and rubbed Olivia's back. "That's why Dad needs some help. You're going to have to go over there and beg Ethan to help."

Olivia knew Audrey was right. If she had to go to Ethan's and beg his forgiveness, she would do it. Anything to save the B&B.

* * *

Ethan and Emma returned home with hardly a word said between them. Emma had a million questions to ask him, but she could tell Ethan wasn't in the mood. He thought of little else but his finances. He was going to have to call the credit-card company and then his bank. He dreaded the thought of having to ask Mrs. Sanderson to pay her bill. He'd almost rather go hungry than do that. But what about the little girl taking a seat at the kitchen table?

His mind was preoccupied, but not enough that he forgot he was responsible for feeding her. He went about fixing her some lunch and set a plate in front of her without a word.

She looked down at the sandwich and then up at him. "What's that?"

His return trip to the refrigerator was cut short and he looked back at her. "What's it look like? It's a bologna sandwich."

She took another look at the two pieces of bread with some sort of "meat" in between. She knew he hadn't bought it at the store earlier so who knows how long it had been sitting in the fridge. She pulled back the top piece of bread so cautiously it looked like she thought a bug would crawl out of the middle. She shook her head and made a face. "I only eat peanut-butter-and-jelly sandwiches."

Ethan's mouth fell open. Had she just told him how it was going to be? Miss White said she could be a little sassy. Probably one of those divas that expect you to wait on them hand and foot. Didn't she understand he was having trouble making ends meet? He guessed the honeymoon period was over.

"Really?"

Emma nodded and scrunched her nose. The smell almost made her sick. "I don't like bologna. Aunt Millie and Uncle Charlie didn't like it either, so we never had it."

Ethan sighed and looked at her. And with those big brown eyes staring back up at him. Like a sad little puppy. How could he counteract that? Back he went to the fridge, loudly moving jars across the shelves in search of some precious jelly. He finally found some.

"I hope you like grape because that's all I got."

The jar had been opened, but he couldn't remember when. A search of the cupboard revealed a half-eaten jar of peanut butter—creamy, not chunky. He plopped down two pieces of bread and lathered a generous helping of peanut butter on one and grape jelly on the other.

"There," he said, putting the plate in front of her.

She looked at the sandwich and then at him.

"What's wrong now?" *Why wasn't she eating the PB&J she just requested?*

"You didn't cut it."

"Oh for the love of Pete."

Emma gasped, her eyes wide. "Aunt Millie says you're not supposed to use swear words."

"I didn't swear."

"But you wanted to, didn't you?"

Ethan grimaced. "This would have been a lot easier if someone had given me a dog."

Her face brightened. "Can we get a dog?"

"No." He noticed her pouting lower lip and sighed. "I don't know. Maybe."

What was he doing?

He swallowed the swear words on the tip of his tongue and went back to the task at hand. He grabbed the knife and then prepared to slice the sandwich in half. He thought better of it and looked at her. His eyebrows rose, begging for a positive response.

She shook her head.

Ethan almost dropped the knife. "What am I doing wrong now?"

"You have to cut it into triangles. Aunt Millie always cut it into triangles."

Ethan's shoulders slumped some more. Really? Was it going to be this hard all of the time? Next thing he knew, she'd probably demand he cut off the crust. He sawed the sandwich as she wished and presented it to her. "There. A peanut-butter-and-jelly sandwich cut into triangles. Now eat it."

Emma took a triangle, looked it over, and then gave it a sniff. Did peanut butter go bad? The jelly smelled like grapes. That was good. She reminded herself to check the expiration date of it and everything else in the fridge and cupboards. She gave it another turn and another sniff. She took a bite.

He raised his eyebrows. "Well?"

Emma shrugged once. "It'll do."

CHAPTER 13

"Geez Louise!"

Ethan's bed shook as he awoke to find Emma standing in front of the nightstand and staring down at him. It was the second morning she had lived with him, but it was the first time she had come into his room. Through his slit eyelids, he thought he saw her wearing a white bathrobe. Didn't she stay in her bedroom yesterday until he was ready to head downstairs for breakfast?

He closed his eyes and asked, "Emma, do you know what day it is?"

"It's Sunday," she said quietly.

His eyes were still too heavy with sleep to open. He had at least another two hours of shut-eye ahead of him, and then he planned on lounging around the house until the Tigers game started after lunch. He was going to have to fill her in on his schedule. He licked his dry lips. "And do you know what we do on Sundays?"

"We go to church."

Ethan's eyes shot wide open. Emma was still standing there next to the bed. He then realized she wasn't wearing a white bathrobe—he should have remembered she didn't have a bathrobe in her garbage bag. Instead, she was wearing her best white dress with a red ribbon in her hair. How long she had been up and getting ready was a mystery to him since she hadn't made a peep.

"The Lord's waiting for us," she said sweetly.

Ethan rose up and rested on an elbow. "He is?" Was he

having another one of those weird dreams?

"Yes. I dusted off your Bible in case you want to take it with you."

Ethan sighed. He couldn't remember the last time he went to church. It must have been shortly after Olivia dumped him. He didn't like the looks he received from people and the whispers behind his back. Of course, they were probably all on her side now that she was a famous actress. Maybe he had just been mad at God and didn't want to go any longer. Whatever the reason, he didn't see any way of getting out of going today. Not with the angel of the morning standing next to his bed.

"How much time do we have?"

"When we drove by your church yesterday, the sign said services start at nine o'clock."

Ethan threw off the covers and sat up. With a quick check of the digital alarm clock, he figured they still had an hour before the service started. Emma was, of course, ready to go.

He rubbed his face and yawned. "You know how to fix cereal, don't you?"

She smiled. "Of course."

Ethan stood up and stretched his arms over his head. "Why don't you fix us a couple bowls of cereal while I get ready."

"Can we have Frosted Flakes?"

"Were they made in Michigan?"

"Oh, yes, in Battle Creek. Says so right on the box. It's the cereal capital of the world."

Ethan gave her nod. "Then we can have Frosted Flakes."

Emma took off like a shot. He couldn't believe the look of glee on her face at the thought of fixing breakfast. "I might be able to get used to this," he whispered to himself.

After a shave and a shower, Ethan rummaged through his closet to find something that would make him look presentable. He decided on a pair of dark slacks, a white dress shirt, and a navy blue tie. When he made it downstairs and into the kitchen, he smiled at what he saw.

"Wow, everything is so very nice."

The bowls of cereal were full and the place settings perfect. The milk was ready to pour, and Emma had a glass of orange juice for each of them.

"Usually, I just eat in front of the TV."

They ate without talking, the only sound being the crunching of the sugary flakes. Once the table was cleared and the teeth were brushed, Ethan and Emma, both in their Sunday best, took the pickup into Huron Cove.

They arrived in the sanctuary with ten minutes to spare, and Ethan started looking for a place to sit.

Emma looked up at him. "Which row is yours?"

"Which row? What do you mean?"

"Which row do you usually sit in? Aunt Millie always sat in the fifth row on the end. That was her spot."

Ethan looked around and thankfully saw most of the regulars must have staked out their pews before the late arrivals.

"It's been awhile since I've been here, Emma. Why don't we pick a spot here in the back."

Ethan took a seat on the end of the back pew and Emma sat close to him. Her head moved all around as she took in the place.

"This is a nice church," she said quietly. She pointed up high above the altar. "That's a big painting of Jesus." She then looked at the inscription above the painting. "Lo, I am with you always."

Ethan looked up at it, too. He vaguely remembered the

verse being there.

"I think that's from Matthew." Emma flipped through the pages. "Aunt Millie taught me to recite all the books of the Bible."

Ethan smiled down at her. "She must have been a wonderful lady."

Emma stopped and ran her finger down the page. "She was. Here it is. Matthew, chapter twenty-eight, verse twenty." She gave the Bible to Ethan so he could read it for himself.

"Yep, there it is. Lo, I am with you always."

"I like that wood carving over the altar. That's Jesus with his disciples at the Last Supper. What's your favorite Bible story? I like Noah and his Ark because of all the animals and the rainbow. Moses parting the Red Sea. David and Goliath. Jonah and the whale, too. And Daniel and the lions' den. Just think how scary that must have been to be locked in the lions' den. And I like Shadrach, Meshach, and Abednego in the fiery furnace. Can you imagine how hot it would be if you were stuck in a fiery furnace? Of course, I like the story of Jesus, too. Who's your favorite disciple? I like Saint Peter. Jesus gave him the keys to the kingdom of heaven. That's pretty cool." She pointed to her left. "That's Saint Peter in that stained-glass window over there. See, he's holding a set of keys."

Ethan couldn't get a word in edgewise. He wondered what had unleashed this torrent of words from Emma. He caught a glimpse from a lady in front of them, who looked back at Ethan and then at Emma. The woman's eyebrows rose and she had to suppress a smile at Ethan's talkative seatmate. With his attention diverted, Ethan didn't see the rest of the parishioners scurrying to find a seat before the organ prelude started the service.

"Hey, look," Emma said, gently tapping Ethan on the

thigh and pointing across the way. "There's your lady friend from yesterday."

Ethan looked over and his heart sank. Why did *she* have to be there? *Not today.* What were the odds? He hadn't figured on seeing Olivia at church, but there she was in the Daniels family spot. The flood of memories washed over him. She looked stunning in her white dress, her long blonde hair resting just beneath her shoulders. Tanned and beautiful, she sat in between her parents and her sisters. Several parishioners leaned forward or turned around to welcome Olivia back to Huron Cove.

"Do you want to go sit by her?"

He waved off the question without a word. He really wanted to leave. He couldn't stop from thinking about how many times he envisioned seeing Olivia walking down the aisle to meet him on their wedding day. She would have been just as stunning then as she was today. Even more so. Married life would see them together in church every Sunday and filling the pews with children. He could feel the sweat dripping down the side of his face. He was glad she didn't show up with a guy on her arm. That would have sent him over the edge.

Thankfully, the service started. Emma seemed to enjoy the songs, followed along intently with the service folder, and hurriedly thumbed through the pages of the Bible for the assigned readings.

Ethan tried to keep his eyes off Olivia, but doggone it if the sun's rays didn't filter through the stained glass and settle right on her like some sort of angelic apparition.

His distracted mind snapped out of it during the sermon when Pastor Carlton mentioned the need to not only love one another, but to forgive one another.

"In Matthew, chapter eighteen, verse twenty-two, Jesus tells us that we must forgive not seven times, but seventy times seven. Thus, forgiving one another is a continuing duty on our part as Christians."

Ethan wondered if he could follow that command. It sounded easy, but it never was. How can you forgive when the love of your life breaks your heart, crushes your soul, and then, to top it all off, never looks back?

Maybe Pastor Carlton had the answer. "And why wouldn't we want to forgive one another? Saint Paul writes in the fourth chapter of Ephesians, verse thirty-two: 'Be kind to each other, tenderhearted, forgiving one another, just as God through Christ has forgiven you.' Just as our sins have been forgiven, let us open our own hearts and forgive those who have wronged us."

During the offering collection, Ethan was shocked back to reality when he opened his wallet and realized he only had the two bucks he found in his dresser that morning. Emma noticed. Thankfully they had gone to the store yesterday. He grabbed the two bills and dropped them into the plate. He hoped his clients would pay their bills tomorrow or he'd be in trouble. Just another thing to worry about.

The service ended with Pastor Carlton's fervent hope that he would see everyone the next Lord's day.

"Okay, let's go," Ethan said to Emma as the worshippers started filing toward the door.

Ethan walked toward the rear doors and thought he would soon be outside and down the sidewalk before Olivia even made it out of her pew. But he wasn't a party of one any longer.

"Well, hello there, Miss Emma," Arlene said. "It's so nice to see you at church."

Ethan clenched his teeth. As much as he wanted to, he couldn't really grab Emma and haul her out of there.

"Thank you," Emma said. "I'm so thankful Mr. Ethan

brought me. It's a very nice church. I like the pipe organ, and I liked Pastor Carlton's sermon."

If Ethan knew anything about the new lady in his life, it was that she could talk until the cows came home. He took a step back and put his arm around her. "It's good to see you, Arlene. Maybe we'll stop in tomorrow for a bite to eat."

Emma's eyes lit up. "I love your chocolate muffins."

Arlene patted her on the shoulder. "Thank you, darling. Aren't you the sweetest thing."

"I'd love to have the recipe so I can bake them someday."

Leaning forward and with a hand on Emma's back, Ethan did his best not to turn around and look for Olivia. He just wanted out of there, so he nudged Emma toward the door. "Okay, we'd better get going. We've got lots to do today."

Ethan took a breath once he and Emma exited the church and hit the sidewalk. They turned left and headed around the building toward the parking lot. When he saw Olivia heading right toward them, for a split second he thought about turning tail and taking the long way around. But he had been spied.

"Oh, man." He could feel his teeth grinding against each other.

"Ethan, hi," Olivia said as she approached.

"Hello." As soon as he said it, his eyes darted away, trying to fixate on anything other than the beautiful Olivia Daniels standing before him. He shifted his feet but went nowhere.

"It's nice to see you again, Ethan. I'm glad you're still going to church."

Ethan didn't tell her that today had been his first day back in a long time. Instead, he nodded. "Yeah."

Feeling the frosty chill in the summer's air, Emma thought she would try to break the ice by stepping forward and extending her hand. "Hi, I'm Emma."

"Well, hello, Emma," Olivia said, reaching out her hand. "I'm Olivia."

Ethan could smell the strawberry-scented conditioner Olivia used. *Oh boy, here come the memories again.*

"I saw you yesterday when you came to Mr. Ethan's house."

Olivia's widening eyes met Ethan's. Did she hear right? This was *the woman* he was hiding in his house yesterday? This sweet little innocent child? Instead of asking for clarification from Emma, Olivia tried her luck with Ethan. "She's staying with you?"

"Yeah."

She pointed at him. "With you?"

Ethan cocked his head and put his hands on his hips. "Yes. Emma here is a cousin of mine. The Department of Child Protective Services came by Friday night and she has been staying with me since then."

Olivia's mouth fell open. "They just stopped by and gave you a child to take care of."

Ethan huffed at the insinuation in her voice. "Yes, as a matter of fact, they did. And I might add that we've been getting along fine. Haven't we, Emma?"

"Oh, yes sir. We've been getting along fine." She smiled in a way that said she meant it.

Olivia still had the look of disbelief on her face. "For how long?"

"I'm not sure," Ethan said, ushering Emma by Olivia. "And now if you'll excuse us, I have to fix peanut-butter-and-jelly sandwiches for lunch."

"Ethan, we still need to talk."

Ethan didn't like it that she used the term "we." There

was no "we" any longer. He turned around, still walking backwards, and pointed at Emma. "Maybe some other time when I'm not so busy."

He finally started to relax as he and Emma hustled down the sidewalk. He was glad to be out of Olivia's orbit. At least for the time being. Now he could go back to trying to forget about her.

Emma, however, wasn't ready just yet. She looked back over her shoulder at Olivia standing on the sidewalk watching them. "Hey, now I know where I've seen her before. She's on TV!"

CHAPTER 14

"Did you know she was on TV?" Emma said as Ethan's pickup rumbled through the streets of Huron Cove.

He hadn't said a word since they got into the truck, although Emma could sense he was thinking about Olivia given how tense his jaw muscles were and how tightly he gripped the steering wheel. The shaking of his head and silent mouthing of words were dead giveaways, too. There was definitely something burning inside of him, and it all had to do with the red-hot flame named Olivia Daniels.

"Yeah, I knew she's been on TV."

Emma's jaw dropped. "You know a real-life TV star?"

Ethan shrugged. "I guess."

"That's so cool. I knew I had seen her before. She's really pretty."

Ethan squeezed the steering wheel tighter, his knuckles turning white. "I think you mentioned that before."

"I like her hair, too. I wish I had hair like that. It's so beautiful."

Ethan grunted his agreement. He had run his fingers through that hair many times. It *was* beautiful. And soft. And lustrous. And radiant. And smelled like strawberries. If his eyes didn't need to stay focused on the road, he would have closed them to let his mind remember the days when he used to hold her close, take in the fragrance of her hair, and then kiss her cherry-red lips.

Snapping out of his trance, Ethan hit the back road on the way home. He wondered how much longer Olivia would be in town. He also wondered how much longer he could take the surprise meetings with her. Maybe he should just move to the other side of Michigan so they'd never bump into each other ever again.

Emma stuck her hand out the window and waved it in the wind. She then turned her attention to Ethan. "She likes you, you know."

Ethan turned to her, his eyes wide. *What in the world brought that on?* He could barely believe she said it. The thought was so funny he busted out laughing. "I don't think so, Emma."

She pulled her hand back inside. "I'm serious. She likes you."

After turning down his lane, Ethan pulled the truck to a stop in the driveway in front of the house and turned off the engine. "No, she doesn't."

Emma sat buckled in her seat, not ready to end the conversation. "She never took her eyes off of you on the sidewalk. And did you see the way she tilted her head? That's a sign that she's interested in you. She did the same thing yesterday when she stopped by the house."

Ethan sat looking across the way at the Daniels' house. "I think you've got it all wrong, Emma. Olivia is not interested in me."

"Did you see how she reached out to brush your arm." Emma demonstrated by reaching over toward Ethan. "That's a sign, too. She wants to be close to you."

Ethan shook his head and chuckled to himself. "How do you know these things?"

Emma looked at him with her big brown eyes. "How else? Oprah."

"Oprah?"

"Yeah, Oprah Winfrey. Aunt Millie and I used to watch her every afternoon after school. I know all about love and relationships. And I can tell Olivia likes you. The signs are all there."

Ethan sighed. He wondered if he should tell Emma about how relationships turn out in the real world. Or how no amount of Oprah can put back the pieces of a shattered heart. He hoped Emma wouldn't bring up Olivia again. She was just a memory now, and a memory he wanted to forget.

He unbuckled his seatbelt and reached for the door. "Come on."

After the two changed out of their Sunday best, Emma followed Ethan around the yard as he made sure it looked immaculate.

"You have a very nice yard," Emma said, holding the rake as Ethan spread the mulch around the flowerbed.

"Thank you. It's what I do for a living. I enjoy being outdoors, and making a yard beautiful makes me feel good. God gave us this huge canvas to work with, and sometimes I feel like an artist when I'm done." He stopped to think for a second. He had surprised himself by mentioning God. Maybe going to church this morning had rubbed off on him.

"It's so quiet and peaceful here. It kind of reminds me of *Anne of Green Gables*."

He picked at a weed and threw it behind him. "That book of yours?"

"Yeah. It's my favorite."

Ethan sat on his knees and looked at her. "What's it about?"

Emma broke into a smile at the question. "It's about a girl named Anne Shirley. She's an orphan and she goes to live with two older people. They're really brother and sister, but they wanted to adopt a boy to help around the farm. They thought about giving her back but she ended up staying with them."

Ethan gave Emma his full attention and listened to her.

"Anne is very smart and she talks a lot and she loves people and she has an active imagination and she's a big dreamer."

"Sounds kind of like someone I know."

"She lives out in the country on Prince Edward Island." She passed the rake to Ethan. "That's up in Canada. Aunt Millie showed it to me on the map. I bet it kind of looks like this." She spread her arms out and looked out over the Huron Cove landscape with its green grass, full trees, and blue water. "Anne becomes friends with a guy named Gilbert, although that doesn't come until later in the book. At first she doesn't like him because he makes fun of her red hair and calls her Carrots. She didn't like that and broke a slate over his head." Emma laughed.

Ethan smiled. "Oh my." He stood up and started moving more of the mulch around. "That sounds like quite the story."

"It was written by L.M. Montgomery. She wrote more books about Anne but I only have the first one."

Ethan looked over the flowerbed and found it presentable. "Grab that bucket." With their tools and buckets in hand, they started walking back toward the white house with the blue accents when Ethan looked at it and had an epiphany. "Maybe I should start calling you Emma of Blue Gables."

Emma's eyes widened. "Really? I could be just like Anne. Oh, I would like that."

Upon hearing Emma's enthusiasm, Ethan regretted saying it. She wasn't his daughter. He had to remind himself that he was single and didn't want a daughter right now. He was a wild, carefree bachelor who lived life to the fullest and wasn't tied down to anyone or anything. He also scolded himself for saying things that might cause Emma to get her hopes up. She would be gone soon. That would be a relief to him. Although he did hope her new home would have colorful gables.

CHAPTER 15

"Olivia, were you able to talk to Ethan after church?" Beth asked.

The Daniels sisters maneuvered around their parents' spacious kitchen as their mother put the finishing touches on the cinnamon rolls for tomorrow's breakfast. It had been an enjoyable day. The entire family started off at church, then had brunch, and now the women sipped iced tea and lemonade while they baked.

Olivia grinned. She had so much to say.

"What?"

"You're not going to believe this." She waited until she caught the attention of Audrey and their mother. "I saw him on the sidewalk after I hustled out of church." Her grin spread across her face. "He was with someone."

Audrey's eyes opened wide. "He brought his girlfriend to church?"

Mrs. Daniels stopped drizzling icing on her pan of cinnamon rolls. "Ethan has a girlfriend? I didn't know that."

"Apparently, she's shacking up with him," Audrey announced like the town gossip. "Is she fat? Ugly?"

Olivia started waving her hands in the air trying to protect Ethan's image for the time being. "No, no, no. I didn't say he was with a woman." She stopped to take a breath. "He was actually with a young girl."

"A child?" Mrs. Daniels asked.

"Yep. Her name is Emma. She looks like she's

probably Bella's age, so I'm guessing eight or nine years old."

Mrs. Daniels wiped her hands on a dish towel. "Have you ever seen the girl before? I don't remember him ever mentioning one."

"Apparently Ethan is related to Emma, and Child Protective Services has given him custody for the time being."

Her mother stood wide eyed. "You're kidding?"

"Nope. He was kind of vague about the whole thing."

Audrey took a seat on the stool at the counter. "That sounds strange. Ethan was always such a party animal in college. Can he even take care of a child?"

Olivia winced. "I don't know. Maybe he has grown up in the last couple of years. All I know is, he was in a hurry to get out of there."

Audrey got up to refill her glass of iced tea. "Did you ask him about working at the B and B?"

Olivia's shoulders sunk and she shook her head. "I still haven't been able to talk to him about it. I can see how uncomfortable he is." She looked out the window toward Ethan's house. "I don't know if he'll do it. Maybe our past is too much to overcome."

Audrey looked over at her younger sister. "Do you still have feelings for him?"

Olivia kept her focus on Ethan's house. So much had happened in the past two years. The awful breakup and her jetting off to California to start a new life. Then Gerard treated her like dirt and left her for his new starlet. Now she was back in Huron Cove for who knows how long. And she needed the help of the man who apparently didn't want anything to do with her.

"I don't know," Olivia said quietly. She looked down at her manicured nails. "I just have so much on my mind, and I want the B and B to survive and thrive. Somehow I have to get Ethan to take the job, even if he can't stand the sight of me. I just don't know how to do it."

Mrs. Daniels sighed. She was going to fix this right here and now. She placed the warm pan of cinnamon rolls in front of Olivia. "I want you to take these rolls to Ethan."

Olivia looked at the pan of cinnamon goodness. "But aren't these for the guests tomorrow?"

"I've got another pan that I can get out of the fridge. If I've learned anything, it's that the quickest way to a man's mind is through his stomach."

"I thought the saying was the quickest way to a man's heart was through his stomach," Audrey said.

"Well, if the rolls make a stop in his heart and his brain, that'll be fine with me." Mrs. Daniels opened up the cupboard and pulled out a plastic container. "Tell him he can store the pan in this container and put it in the fridge. Then tomorrow all he has to do is warm them up in the oven."

"Okay, thanks Mom."

"And why don't you take Bella with you. Maybe you can introduce her to Emma and they can play while you and Ethan talk."

* * *

After a lunch of peanut-butter-and-jelly triangle sandwiches, Ethan and Emma retired to the living room so they could watch the afternoon matchup between the Tigers and the Yankees on TV. Although Emma kept her copy of *Anne of Green Gables* nearby, she focused her attention squarely on the ball game. She even commented on the poor state of the Tigers' defense given the team's four errors through the first five innings. Down by eight runs, Ethan couldn't stop shaking his head.

"Looks like the Tigers didn't come to play today, Emma. They must have had a late night yesterday."

Ethan tossed a baseball into the air as he relaxed on the couch. He seemed to always have a baseball in his hand when he was growing up, and it was a habit for him to toss it toward the ceiling to pass the time. The well-worn leather baseball glove on his left hand had probably caught that same ball a thousand times. Emma took notice.

"You know, I can play catch if you want."

Ethan's baseball didn't make a return trip toward the ceiling. He turned his head toward Emma sitting in the recliner. "You can?"

Emma smiled and nodded. "Yep. I used to play at Aunt Millie's. Her neighbors liked to play wiffle ball, and sometimes they'd let me come over and play. I can throw to you if you want."

Ethan could see the look in Emma's eyes. She wanted to play. He took a look at the screen again just in time to see the Tigers' shortstop throw the ball over the first baseman's head and into the stands. "Well, Emma, I think I'd rather play catch with you than watch this."

Ethan dug around the shelves in the garage and found an older glove for Emma to use. It was too big for her hand but it would do the job. They walked out into the yard beside the house and stood thirty feet apart.

Ethan patted the palm of his glove twice. "Okay, Emma, let's see what you've got."

Emma wound up and with a little grunt fired a chest-high strike that popped into Ethan's glove. He returned the throw and was impressed that she caught the ball with two hands. She wound up again and threw another strike to Ethan.

"Hey, you're pretty good for . . ."

Emma caught the return throw as well as Ethan's

inability to finish his sentence. "You mean for a girl."

Ethan smiled and shrugged. "Well, yeah."

Ethan and Emma played catch for a good ten minutes. Ethan told her about playing baseball in college, and Emma told him how Aunt Millie was a big fan of Tiger great Al Kaline. When the conversation ended, Ethan couldn't help but think about what he was doing—playing catch with his pretend daughter. Who would have dreamed that up three days ago? He realized he had dreamt of one day playing catch with a son, but having Emma tossing the ball back and forth didn't disappoint him.

With the ball in hand, Emma took a step back looking like she was preparing to throw the final pitch of the World Series. In the middle of her windup, she caught a glimpse of a blonde-haired woman and a young girl crossing the lawn toward them. "Hey look. There's Miss Olivia."

With a quick turn of his head, Ethan never saw the ball heading right for him. It hit him with a thud in the right biceps. "Ow."

Emma dropped her glove and ran to him. "Mr. Ethan, are you okay? I'm so sorry. I thought you were looking. I'm so sorry."

Ethan reached out his sore right arm and patted her on the shoulder. "It's okay, Emma. It doesn't hurt that bad. Probably should have been paying attention."

Emma reached up to help rub the hurt out of Ethan's arm. "I'm really sorry."

Ethan flexed his arm a couple of times and announced he was good as new. "Really, it's okay. I'll have to remember to keep an eye out for your fastball next time."

Emma smiled in relief.

Ethan's concern over his arm quickly turned to Olivia making her way across the grass. She was carrying something. Probably a peace offering. And the little girl with her held a soccer ball under her arm. He kind of wished Emma had hit him in the head with her fastball instead of his arm. Maybe it would have knocked him out so he wouldn't have to deal with Olivia.

Olivia waved when they crossed the property line. "Hi, Ethan."

Ethan wiped some sweat off his forehead. "Hi."

"My mom made you some of her famous cinnamon rolls."

Ethan didn't offer to take the container off her hands. He stood there, his left hand rubbing his right biceps.

"Hi, Emma, how are you doing?"

Emma smiled broadly. A real life actress was talking to her! "I'm fine, Miss Olivia. It's nice to see you again. I've seen you on TV."

Olivia flashed her megawatt smile. "Emma, this is my niece, Bella." She put her free arm around her niece's shoulder.

"Hi," Emma said, waving.

Olivia encouraged Bella under her breath to say something.

"Would you like to play soccer?" Bella asked.

Emma looked up at Ethan, who just then realized he was about to lose his wingman (or maybe it was wingwoman) and would have to deal with Olivia all by himself. He nodded that it was okay, and Emma and Bella took off.

"Make sure you stay where I can see you, Emma," Ethan said. He gave Olivia a look that said, *See, I'm responsible.*

"Can we sit on the steps, Ethan?"

Ethan sighed but relented.

They each took a seat on the top step, both of them up

against the opposite railing from each other. Ethan kept his focus on the two girls as Emma kicked the soccer ball over Bella's head.

Olivia broke the ice. "Emma looks like she might be an athlete someday."

Ethan watched Emma sprint after the ball to retrieve it. "You might be right."

The light wind blew the leaves in the trees. Ethan couldn't remember the last time he had been alone with Olivia on these steps. He remembered the first time, though. They were ten years old, and even at that young age, Ethan knew Olivia Daniels was a stunner. She had been the picture of youthful beauty—long golden blonde hair and eyes as blue as Lake Huron. She was the one to make the first move, and a quick peck on the cheek to her fifth-grade classmate was the first of many in their school-age romance.

"Were you two playing catch?"

Ethan snapped out of his daydream and looked at Olivia. He nodded twice and then returned his gaze toward Emma. "She's got quite an arm." He wondered if his biceps would have a bruise tomorrow. "And she's got good control, too."

Olivia realized she was going to have to make the first move this time around, too. She took a deep breath. "Ethan, I need your help." She didn't pause to let him respond. "I've hit the wall in Hollywood. I haven't had a paying job in almost a year, and it's not going to get any easier out there. So I've decided to move back to Huron Cove to run the B and B. Mom and Dad can't run it forever, and Dad is having a hard time keeping it up to his high standards."

Ethan didn't look at her while she continued.

"It's something I've always thought I would do

someday." She turned her eyes toward Emma and Bella. "I guess it's a little sooner than I thought." She then glanced down at her beautifully manicured hands. "I want to start booking weddings again like we did when I was younger. And maybe we could have family reunions here, too. But I'm going to need help."

Ethan looked down to the bottom step, his mind lost in thought.

Olivia thought she was going to have to pull out all the stops. "What are you going to do with Emma when you have to go to work tomorrow?"

Ethan's head turned toward Olivia and his nostrils flared. He didn't know. He hadn't even considered it. But he thought he'd figure something out. He didn't need Olivia.

"Ethan, I can help with Emma. She can come over to our house and play with Bella during the day. My sisters and Mom would be glad to watch over her and get to know her. She seems like such a sweetheart."

Ethan's teeth were grinding together. He rotated his stiff neck trying to lessen the tension. How could he work alongside someone who left him for the dreams of Hollywood and the arms of Gerard Cologne? He wanted to say he couldn't and wouldn't do such a thing. But it was then that he remembered dropping the last two dollars in his wallet to the collection plate at church that morning. He and Emma couldn't survive on triangle PB&Js forever. But letting Olivia back into his life?

"I'm sure Bella and Emma will . . ."

Ethan cut her off. "I need the money, Olivia." He was still looking down at the ground. He didn't feel ashamed about saying it, he was simply trying to short-circuit any further pleading from Olivia. "I'll do it for the money. And I'll do it for Emma. That's all."

Olivia didn't take her eyes off of him. She took in the strong jaw line, the muscular physique. He was even more handsome now than she remembered. Maybe because she needed him now more than ever. She was relieved that he accepted her offer, if only for monetary reasons. It was a start. A first step on the road to forgiveness. And who knows where that road would take them.

CHAPTER 16

Perhaps it was the Michigan sunrise or maybe it was the smell of Mrs. Daniels's cinnamon rolls, but Ethan was in a particularly good mood that Monday morning. He walked downstairs to see the table set for breakfast and Emma hard at work.

"Where'd you find that apron, Emma?"

Emma looked down at the front of the blue apron and its gold outline of Michigan. "I found it in that drawer over there. I hope it's okay for me to wear it."

Ethan smiled and nodded. The apron was much too big for her, so she had to tie it behind her and then in front and curl the garment underneath so she didn't trip over it. The bowls were filled with Frosted Flakes and separate plates held the warm cinnamon rolls.

"Did you warm these in the oven?"

"Yes. I thought about using the microwave, but Aunt Millie taught me how to use the oven." She pointed to the stainless steel appliance. "Don't worry, though. I've turned it off now."

Ethan smiled. "This is some spread you've fixed this morning. You are quite the chef."

Emma placed the newspaper next to him at the table. "The Tigers ended up losing by nine," she announced as if that matter of business was important for Ethan to digest while he ate his meal.

"Yeah, we could kind of see that one coming."

The two sat down to eat, and Ethan commented how

good everything tasted. He thought Emma seemed to be enjoying herself.

"How do you like Bella?" Ethan asked her between bites.

"I like her. It's nice to have someone near my own age."

"You think you two can get along while I work at the B and B today?"

"Oh yes. We'll get along fine."

"Okay. I just want you to know that I'll be around if you need anything. Just ask Mrs. Daniels and she'll find me."

The pair cleaned the table and washed up. Ethan tied his work boots and grabbed a pair of leather gloves. Emma wore her shorts and her pink Minion tank top.

Ethan looked at his watch and then at Emma. "Time to go to work."

They walked across the grass, still wet with dew, and met Olivia and Bella on the front porch of the Daniels residence.

"Hi, Emma," Olivia said.

"Hi, Miss Olivia. Hi, Bella."

Bella hopped down the steps and grabbed Emma's hand. "Let me go show you my room."

With that the two girls were off to play, which left Ethan and Olivia to stand and stare awkwardly at each other.

"Hi," Olivia said.

Ethan actually kept his eyes on her for once. "Morning." It was more of a businesslike greeting.

Olivia walked down the steps toward him. "Ready to get to work."

Ethan still hadn't taken his eyes off of her. She wore a red-and-white checkerboard button down top that was tied in a knot at her midriff. Everything about her sparkled. The designer jeans, which probably cost about as much as Ethan's monthly wages, were ripped in all the right places and most likely added a few hundred dollars to the price. She could have been preparing for a photo shoot for a high-end clothing company.

Not preparing to work in the yard.

Ethan shook his head slightly. She was still the beautiful Olivia Daniels he had always known. "First thing we have to do is get you out of those pants."

Olivia tilted her head and put a hand on her hip. "Excuse me? That's a bit forward of you, isn't it, Ethan? Aren't you supposed to buy me dinner first?"

Ethan's face turned apple red. "I . . . um . . . I didn't mean it that way. I . . . um . . . I just meant that you might be getting dirty and might want to change your clothes to something more . . . or I mean. . . something less . . . expensive."

Olivia sighed and rolled her eyes. "Fine. I'll be right back."

It took her surprising little time to change her clothes and she came back outside wearing a tight-fitting maize and blue Michigan Wolverine T-shirt and denim overalls. Ethan had to restrain himself from mouthing a "wow." The clothes must have been hers because they hugged every curve she had. She still didn't look ready for yard work, but it was the best she could do.

They both looked at each other wondering who should speak first. It had been awhile since they were totally alone. When they were in love, she used to jump into his embrace and he would twirl her around and around. Today it was just business.

"Well," Ethan said. "You're the boss. What do you want me to do?"

Olivia led them toward the barn. "I want to refurbish the barn for wedding receptions. When we had weddings when I was little, we just had the happy couple and friends out on the beach. Then they had to go to the country club for the reception. I think we could be a one-stop shop for the wedding parties if we fix up the barn."

Olivia stopped at the barn doors. She gave the door and the surrounding buildup of weeds a good once over before she turned her head toward Ethan.

He shook his head and rolled his eyes. "Didn't bring your work gloves, did you?"

Ethan beat a path to the door and, after a few pulls and pushes on the rusty wheels, he forced the barn doors open. The cool dusty air hit them both in the face. Ethan swatted away some cobwebs and then motioned for Olivia to follow him.

"What do you think?" Olivia asked.

"You've got the design ideas. You tell me."

Olivia's eyes widened as she spouted off her dreams. "Just imagine these hardwood floors refinished and the exposed beams painted. There would be tables over there and the dance floor in the middle. Flowers and lights. It would be such a beautiful setting."

A large part of Ethan couldn't believe he was standing next to Olivia talking about wedding receptions. He couldn't believe a lot of things lately. He bent down, grabbed an old board with rusty nails, and tossed it to the side.

Olivia watched him. "Do you think you can do the job?"

Ethan took a step forward and started gauging the time and effort to make the barn look pristine and perfect. "Well, I'm more of the landscape guy, but I think I could do it. I would have to start by cleaning out everything.

Then there would be a lot of sanding and staining. I might have to find some help on that front, but I think I could have this place looking like a mountain chalet in a matter of weeks. You'd probably have to hire an electrician, though, for any special lighting you want. You might want to consider a projection screen and an audio system. I can obviously do the grounds surrounding the barn as well."

Olivia's starry eyes told Ethan her answer but she said it anyway. "That's what I want to do."

"Okay. What else?"

Olivia backed out of the barn and looked across the property. "We'll have to fix up the landscape around the gazebo, too. That way the bridal party can have pictures taken there. And the B and B guests can use it too for relaxing."

Ethan took his mental notes as they walked. "What else?"

With the gazebo now on the list, Olivia walked toward the beach. "Before we do any of this, I think we need to get ready for the Fourth of July fireworks. We'll need to clear the beach and the area surrounding the lighthouse. I've already put in a call to city hall to get the permits for the fireworks. My dad has also contacted a buddy of his who has the barge to launch them."

"Okay."

Once they walked through the opening of the split rail fence and stepped onto the beach, Olivia stopped to take it all in. She held up her hands, her thumbs together, and looked at the surrounding landscape through her makeshift viewfinder. "Just imagine it. Hundreds of families enjoying an evening on the beaches of Lake Huron. Maybe we could have live music with a patriotic flare. The band could use the pier to play from. And we'd have hot dogs, and apple pie, and Coca-Cola. Then the fireworks to cap off the night."

Ethan could hear the passion in her voice. She used to get that way when she talked about acting and her dreams of making it onto the big screen.

"Wouldn't that be wonderful?"

Ethan caught a glimpse of her out of the corner of her eye. She was smiling that award-winning smile. "Sure sounds like it."

They continued walking toward the lighthouse. Olivia spread her arms again. "Just imagine the fireworks with the lighthouse in the foreground. It will be so picturesque. And once the fireworks celebration is over, think of the weddings that we can schedule. I think I should hire a photographer to capture it all for the website and the brochure."

Once they neared the large rocks around the lighthouse, Ethan stopped in his tracks while Olivia kept walking and jabbering on about her plans. Perhaps it was the blonde hair or the smooth skin kissed by the Southern California sun or maybe just the sweet sound of her voice, but his heart started pounding and he felt like he was going to hyperventilate. He closed his eyes and tried to take a deep breath.

All he could think about was this was the spot of their very first "real" kiss. The deep sensual kind that lovers remember for the rest of their lives. This was the spot where he had told her he loved her.

"Ethan, did you hear me?"

He could feel his insides tying themselves into a knot. She apparently didn't have the same recall. He shook his head after he thought he heard the name Emma. "What?"

"I said I bet Emma would like to see the fireworks."

Emma. Yes, she was the reason he was doing this. She was the reason why he was trailing the woman who broke his heart and willing to work for her.

"Ethan?"

Ethan took a step forward. "Yeah," he said softly. "I bet Emma would love to see them."

He couldn't believe she was so nonchalant about where they were. Maybe Hollywood had wiped out the memories of what happened right here just a couple of years ago. This was the spot where he got down on bended knee and proposed to the love of his life.

And it was also the spot where she said no.

CHAPTER 17

"Did you know that Thomas Edison lived in the Thumb region of Michigan when he was a boy?" Emma asked as she flipped through her new book of Michigan facts given to her by her new best friend Bella.

Ethan had a firm grip on the steering wheel and hadn't said a word as they drove into Huron Cove. He was trying to forget about the day. "I guess that's better than being from the middle finger region."

Emma looked up from her book and corrected him. "Michigan is a mitten, not a glove. So there's no middle finger, just a thumb."

"Oh. Sorry. I guess it just feels like life is giving me the finger sometimes."

Emma closed her book. "You want to talk about it?"

Ethan rubbed the back of his neck. If Emma wasn't here, he probably would have been heading into Huron Cove to meet up with Curt at the nearest watering hole and drown his sorrows in drink. He didn't take his eyes off the road. "Are you pulling out your Oprah again?"

She smiled, looked outside her window, and thought of something to say. "You're supposed to talk about your feelings."

"Why would I want to talk about my feelings to other people?"

"Because it'll make you feel better than to keep them all bottled up inside of you. Kind of like a balloon filled with air about ready to burst. If you let out some of the air, it's less likely to pop."

Ethan couldn't argue with that logic. He turned into the drive-thru at the bank and waited for the car in front of him to move. "Olivia and I used to be pretty close." There was no enthusiasm in his voice, just the dejected memory of a lost love.

"Did you love her?"

Ethan looked over at Emma and nodded. "Yeah. I loved her a lot."

Ethan had never said that to another person. Curt would have found a way to make fun of him somehow. But, boy, did he ever love Olivia Daniels.

"Did you tell her you loved her?"

"I told her I loved her many times." He stopped talking as he pulled up to the window and waited for the teller.

"Can I help you?"

"I'd like to cash these checks, please." He dropped the checks into the drawer.

As the teller totaled up the checks, Emma continued. "But she left and went to Hollywood with some guy, didn't she?"

Ethan turned his head and gave a good hard look at Emma. He gritted his teeth while he tried to think of something to say. "How do you know all of this?"

Emma gave a slight smile. "I ask a lot of questions."

Ethan chuckled. "Yes, you do."

"But it's just natural curiosity. How else am I going to learn?"

"Well, don't believe all the gossip, Emma. Who'd you hear this from?"

"Mrs. Daniels and Bella's mom. We talked about you and Olivia when we had lunch. We had egg salad sandwiches, and Mrs. Daniels even cut them into triangles for me and Bella. Anyway, I just wanted to know a little bit more about you so I asked them."

Ethan grabbed the envelope full of cash from the box and thanked the teller. He drove forward, looked both ways, and then turned left onto Main Street.

"How about some pizza, Emma? You do like pizza, don't you?"

"Oh, yes. I like it very much. I like all kinds of toppings, except for anchovies and mushrooms."

"I don't like anchovies or mushrooms either, but they have good pizza here." Ethan pulled to a stop in front of Rose's Pizzeria. As he held the door for her, he noted. "And they cut the pieces into triangles, too."

With a large pepperoni pizza and some Cokes to wash it down, Ethan and Emma sat in front of the window that looked out at Main Street.

"Would you like to say grace, Emma?"

Emma responded with a bright smile. "Oh yes, I'd love to. We used to say grace all the time at Aunt Millie and Uncle Charlie's." She folded her hands and bowed her head. "Dear Lord, thank you for bringing us to Rose's Pizzeria. Just as you created the heavens and the earth and found it to be 'very good,' we thank you for making pepperoni pizza which looks and smells so very good, too."

Ethan opened his eyes to sneak a peek. He smiled at her seriousness and closed his eyes again.

"Amen."

"Thank you, Emma." Ethan put a slice of pizza on a plate and passed it over. "Be careful, it's nice and hot."

Emma grabbed a shaker of Parmesan cheese and frosted the top of her slice. She took a bite and smiled at Ethan.

"It's good, isn't it?"

"Very good." She put down her slice and took a drink.

Discussion time. "Mr. Ethan, I think Olivia still likes you."

She just wouldn't let it go. Why she wouldn't, he didn't know. "What's it to you?"

Emma wiped her mouth with her napkin. "I want you to be happy. I know you love her, and I think she wants to love again."

Ethan sat back in his chair. He let out a deep breath and pointed his index finger at her. "Correction. I loved her. Past tense. She moved on, and I've moved on, too."

"Have you?"

If she had a pair of half glasses and a notepad in front of her, he might think she was some shrink intent on studying his mind. He was thankful to get the job at the B&B. It would pay well. But he thought it would be a short-time gig and maybe sporadic thereafter. Whatever the case, Olivia Daniels wasn't going to be a part of his life much longer.

"Olivia will probably be going back to Hollywood pretty soon. She loves the bright lights of the big city and being the center of attention. She'll be gone from our lives and we'll only see her on TV."

CHAPTER 18

With Ethan hard at work at the B&B, Olivia hoped to use her people skills to spread the word about the upcoming fireworks show. So, with her overalls left behind, she stepped out of her Mustang in a down-home but stylish pair of jeans and red checkerboard shirt. With a handful of flyers, she stopped off at the Food Mart, the hardware store, and the Post Office.

At her last stop, she opened the door to The Coffee Cove and heard the familiar bell ring her appearance.

"Good morning, Arlene," she said, heading toward the counter.

Arlene gave her a broad smile. "Olivia, so nice to see you." She walked out from behind the counter to give Olivia a hug. She then pointed to the wall. "Look, I've put up the photo that you signed for me. The Coffee Cove's most famous employee. It's like you have your own wall of fame."

Olivia thought the wall needed a little more fame, what with it only having her photo amongst the pictures of lighthouses and other Michigan paraphernalia. She thanked Arlene for the sweet gesture and took a seat at the counter.

"What can I get you?"

"I'll just have a small coffee, Arlene. I've been dropping off flyers for the fireworks show."

"I heard you were the reason for the show going on."

"Summer in Huron Cove just wouldn't be the same without fireworks. I was hoping I could leave some by the cash register."

Arlene handed a cup across the counter. "Of course. Anything I can do to help. How is the preparation for the Fourth coming along?"

"It's going pretty well. We still have a lot of work to do to make it all happen?"

"*We*?"

Olivia caught the underlying tone of Arlene's question. She hid a slight smile crossing her lips with a sip of coffee. "I was able to convince Ethan to work for the B and B. He's not only helping with the fireworks show, he's also going to be doing a lot of work for the weddings I'm hoping to have someday."

"And Ethan's okay with this arrangement?"

Olivia looked away—toward the window not her wall of fame. "I'm not sure he's totally comfortable with it, but at least it's a step in the right direction."

Arlene lowered her voice so the other customers couldn't hear. "It was hard on him when you left."

Olivia caught the seriousness in Arlene's eyes and nodded. She had been too busy chasing her dreams in Hollywood to think much about the broken dreams she had left behind in Huron Cove. She knew that coming back would require her to mend a lot of fences, especially with Ethan.

"It all happened so fast, Arlene. One minute I'm a theater student in Ann Arbor and the next I'm on a plane to Los Angeles with Gerard for a casting call. I know I didn't end things well with Ethan. He deserved better than that. I was just young and didn't know any better."

Arlene may have loved Olivia like a daughter, but she also loved Ethan like a son. "He was really down in the dumps, moping around town for I don't know how long. That was if he even showed his face at all. A lot of us were worried about him. I think he even stopped going to church."

Olivia's shoulders sagged. "That's what my mom said. I hate it that I caused him any pain. It's not that I didn't love him. It's just . . ." This time her gaze took her to her publicity shot on the wall. It had been all about her and her career. Ethan couldn't offer her name in lights, but Gerard promised her the world. That was all she needed, and she dumped Ethan without even looking back. She sighed.

Arlene gave her a few seconds. "Do you still love him?"

Olivia looked at Arlene and then settled her eyes on her coffee cup. Did she still love Ethan Stone? Is that really why she came back? Or was it to seek the safety and security of home and family after Gerard discarded her for the newest blonde superstar that came his way?

"I don't know." She thought about it some more. "I mean. I guess I still have feelings for him, but I don't know whether he could love me again. I want to be with someone who loves me with all their heart. And I don't know whether Ethan can do that because of what I did to him."

Arlene refilled Olivia's cup. It appeared like it could be a two-cup discussion. "Ethan's grown up some since you left. He and Curt still spend too much time going out to howl at the moon. But that might be the product of a broken heart. Even though there are plenty of women on the prowl, he hasn't been seeing anyone that I know of. I'm afraid he might be too damaged to want to start a relationship right now." She gave Olivia a pat on the arm. "But have you seen that little angel of a girl he's got following him around? Oh my, what a darling."

Olivia smiled, her mood brightening. "I've met Emma. She's a bit of a sparkplug. Very talkative. Smart, too."

Arlene laughed. "I can only imagine what it must be like in the Ethan Stone household these days. A week ago, he was a wild horse roaming free. Now he's got an eight-year-old girl to take care of. I bet she's got him wrapped around her little finger."

"You think?"

"Absolutely. You know Ethan has always had a big heart. And behind that handsome exterior, he's just a big softy."

Olivia looked out the window. She remembered the times when they would hold hands on the beach or at the movie theater. She loved it when he would slip her notes in class or after church telling her how much he loved her. She still had the notes, the cards, even the poems he wrote for her tucked away in some shoe box in her old bedroom. Was he the one for her? Was she willing to find out?

"Maybe you ought to see if he's ready to love again, Olivia. It would be good for him. And it might end up being good for the both of you."

"What if he's not ready?"

Arlene shrugged and shook her head. "Well, maybe it's not the right time."

Olivia took the statement to heart.

"But if he is ready," Arlene said, pointing a finger at her. "Make sure you're ready, too. Because you don't want to break his heart again. I don't know if he could handle it."

Olivia got up from her stool and raised her cup. "Thanks for the coffee, Arlene. And the conversation."

CHAPTER 19

"I really love living here," Emma said. "It's such a beautiful area."

As Bella's newest friend, Emma had quickly become a part of the Daniels' extended family. Ethan would walk her over every day when it was time for him to go to work. It worked out best for both of them—she had a friend to play with and he knew she was in good hands.

For the Daniels' part, they loved having Emma in their lives. She was an endless font of energy and discussion, and her sweetness made her a joy to have around.

"Well, we're glad you like it here," Mrs. Daniels said.

The kitchen smelled of fresh baked chocolate chip cookies, as Mrs. Daniels, Bella, and Emma, each in their aprons, prepared another batch for the oven.

"And how do you like living with Ethan?"

Emma's eyes sparkled. "Oh, I really like staying with Mr. Ethan. We went out for pizza the other night. We had pepperoni. I don't like anchovies or mushrooms, and he doesn't either. Then we came back to the house and watched the Tigers on TV." She frowned. "They lost. Again."

The door to the kitchen opened and Olivia walked in.

"Hi, Aunt Olivia," Bella said. "We're making cookies."

Olivia smiled and gave hugs to Bella and Emma. "I could smell the goodness before I even walked in the door. You ladies look like you've been working hard."

Mrs. Daniels closed the oven door after sliding in the sheet. "We've made three dozen already. Two more are in the oven. That ought to feed the guests and everybody else in town for a good while. What have you been up to?"

Olivia took a seat at the breakfast bar. "I was passing out flyers for the fireworks display. I stopped at all the local businesses and even passed some out on the street. People seem excited about it."

"I'm excited about it!" Emma said. "I've never been to a real fireworks show. Aunt Millie and I used to watch the fireworks in Washington, D.C. on TV every Fourth of July. They were always so pretty with the patriotic music."

Olivia smiled. She hoped she could bring some joy to Emma's life. "We're going to have a concert to go along with the fireworks. There will be plenty of patriotic tunes. And Mr. Butler at the Food Mart said he would provide the hot dogs and buns for all who come hungry."

Mrs. Daniels put the empty cookie dough bowl into the sink. "Do you think you'll have the beach and lighthouse ready for everyone?"

Olivia looked out the window. "I'll have to talk to Ethan. I know he was going to be working on the barn floors today. It shouldn't be too much to get the beach cleaned up. The flyers tell people to bring their lawn chairs and blankets."

Mrs. Daniels took off her apron. "Speaking of Ethan, we were just talking about him. Emma says she really likes living with him."

Emma nodded her head and smiled.

Mrs. Daniels looked at her daughter. "So, how have you two been getting along?"

Olivia didn't want to say much in front of Emma, hoping not to hurt her feelings or give her cause for concern. The ice between Olivia and Ethan had begun to thaw, but it looked like it was going to take time. "We've been getting along just fine. I think he's excited about the B and B projects. I know he'll do a great job turning it into a showplace that brides and grooms will flock to once it's done."

* * *

Emma took notice of the pained look in Olivia's eyes. It was the same look Ethan had whenever the name Olivia was mentioned in conversation. Sometimes it looked and sounded like it was going to take a miracle to bring them back together.

Or maybe all it would take was a little angel and some chocolate chip cookies.

"Maybe we should take Mr. Ethan some cookies for lunch!" Emma said.

Mrs. Daniels brought her hands together. "I think that is a wonderful idea, Emma. Why don't you and Olivia take some cookies to Ethan while Bella and I take some to grandpa."

Emma took a bag of cookies and Olivia took a bottled water. Once they hit the front porch, Emma went to work.

"Mr. Ethan is so wonderful to live with, Miss Olivia. He is super nice, and we have a lot of fun together."

Curious at the little girl's exuberance, Olivia asked, "What kind of fun things do you two do?"

"We watch the Tigers and we play catch. Last night, we fixed macaroni and cheese and then we did the laundry."

"The laundry?"

"Yeah, I don't have many clothes so we have to do the laundry every couple of days. Mr. Ethan said he's going to take me to the store to buy me some more things to wear. And we have breakfast together and read the paper. I always tell him the standings in the American League. I try not to tell him the Tigers are in last place in the central but he already knows."

"Ethan was always a huge Tigers fan when he was growing up. He and my dad even went to a couple of games."

"Did he go to games with his parents?"

"Oh, I think they went to a few, but they were always working and Ethan was playing baseball so there wasn't a lot of free time. Then his parents passed away a couple of years ago."

Emma looked up at Olivia. "That's sad. I know what it's like to be sad when it comes to that." She looked at the barn in front of her. "I don't want Mr. Ethan to be sad."

Olivia slowed and put her arm around Emma's shoulders. "I don't want Ethan to be sad either, Emma."

Emma smiled. She was glad to hear it. "Maybe these cookies will make him happy."

* * *

The warm Michigan summer had raised the temperature in the Daniels' barn, and Ethan felt the heat as he sanded the wood floor to its original look. He had been at it since seven that morning, and he hoped to stain the floor tomorrow. He had to admit, Olivia had an eye for design. Once the floors were done and the new lighting installed, the barn would be a spectacular venue for a wedding reception. After unplugging the cord to the sander, his attention was drawn to the two people in the doorway to the barn.

"Well, look who's here."

Emma held up the bag of goodies. "Hi, Mr. Ethan, we brought you some cookies."

Ethan walked over to them and wiped the perspiration

off his forehead. His white T-shirt clung to his muscular chest and accentuated all his pectorals and biceps.

"My mom and the girls made a whole bunch of chocolate chip cookies. We brought you some water, too."

Ethan smiled and thanked them. He took the water from Olivia first and quenched his thirst. Then he turned and showed them his work while he snacked on a cookie. "I think the floor is going to turn out great. It'll shine like glass once I get finished with it."

"It really is looking wonderful, Ethan," Olivia said. "You have done amazing work."

"Thanks."

"And the lawn is looking fabulous as well."

Not one to bask in adulation, Ethan patted Emma on the shoulder. "I had some help last night. Emma has a green thumb." He smiled at her. "And she has a good landscaping eye."

Not only did she have a green thumb and a landscaper's eye, she also had the wherewithal to know when two people might need a moment alone. She walked over to the belt sander and pretended to be enthralled with its mechanics.

"She really is something, Ethan," Olivia whispered so only he could hear.

Ethan nodded as he looked at Emma reach up to pretend to drive the sander. "That she is."

"Everyone at my parents' house loves her. She's fit in like a member of the family."

Ethan didn't respond. He brought the bottle of water to his lips and took a drink. He had been so busy the last couple of days with work and with Emma that he had forgotten all about his temporary custody of her. He had to remind himself not to get too attached, which was a hard thing to do with such a sweet angel. But it had to be done.

Otherwise, his heart would be broken again. By the same token, he had to keep the wall up between him and Olivia. She would be gone soon, too. Back to Hollywood to live the life she always dreamed of. He wasn't going to let her break his heart again.

Olivia looked at him, as if waiting for him to say something. The tension between them caused him to step away.

He didn't look at either of them as he looked for his broom. "Thanks for the cookies, ladies. But I had better get back to work."

CHAPTER 20

The drive into Huron Cove felt strange to Ethan for one undeniable reason. It was quiet. He heard little but the wind rushing in through the open window. It seemed like a lifetime ago when he had the truck to himself and his thoughts. But the seat next to him was empty, and thus he was deprived of the endless stream of Michigan facts and other eight-year-old musings he had grown accustomed to hearing. He chuckled to himself. He missed Emma.

After a long hard day of sanding and staining the barn floor, Ethan thought he would have a quiet restful night at home. Maybe cook some steaks and potatoes and watch a little baseball with Emma. But Emma got a better offer—her first ever slumber party with Bella. Ethan could hardly deprive Emma of an overnight with her new friend. Although he planned on taking to the couch and resting for the evening, a call from Curt to head out on the town changed his mind.

"There's the man!" Curt said over the boisterous crowd of The Cellar. "It's about time you get out on the town again. What are you drinking?"

"Just a ginger ale tonight."

"Ginger ale! You need a little something stronger than that. Have all those women corrupted your mind or what?"

Ethan gave his buddy a smile and shook his head. "I'm driving tonight. Plus, I don't feel like staying out late."

Curt ran his hands down his face in despair. "I can't believe it. The wild horse Ethan Stone has been saddled and domesticated."

Ethan took the glass of ginger ale from the waitress. "I haven't been domesticated. I just have a lot of things going on right now."

Curt pointed toward the corner. "Let's get a table. Tigers are already down by three in the top of the first." Once seated, Curt said, "So, how's the babysitting going?"

"It's not all bad. She's got a lot of spunk. She talks a lot, but I don't mind."

"So, what, you have to change her diapers and feed her?"

Ethan's eyes widened and his mouth fell open. Did his single friend have no clue? Even Ethan knew better than that. "She's eight years old, Curt. She doesn't need diapers or have to be fed. She can actually cook some, probably more if I ever had something in the fridge. And she washes dishes and makes her bed and folds laundry. Articulate little thing, too. Somebody must have raised her right because she can spout off on just about anything."

Curt raised his eyebrows like he thought it sounded like a good deal. "Maybe I ought to get one of those kids to work at my place." He dug into the hot wings before the waitress could even put the plate on the table. "When are they going to take her off your hands so you can get your bachelor pad back?"

Ethan looked at the TV, but it wasn't to check the score of the ball game. Any question or even the thought of Emma going away caused a twinge in his gut. He wasn't sure why it happened or when it first started. She was going to have to leave for a real home one of these days. And it would be best if it were sooner rather than later—less painful for all involved. *That's what he wanted, wasn't it?*

"I haven't heard from Miss White from Ann Arbor since she dropped Emma off."

Did Miss White even give him her phone number? If so, where did he put it?

"You're not thinking about keeping her, are you?"

"Of course not," Ethan blurted out before his conscience could say otherwise. He rubbed a napkin in his hands. *He didn't want to keep her, did he?* He had thought someday he would get married and have children—his own children. Not one thrust upon him late one Friday night.

Curt chomped down on another wing. "That's good to hear. You don't want to be weighed down by some kid when you're out looking for a woman. They might think an eight-year-old child is too much to take on. It'll only get worse once she hits her teen years. Free and unattached is the way to go, my friend."

Ethan didn't respond. Curt probably hadn't heard that from Oprah. Ethan looked at the basket of wings but didn't feel like eating. He wanted to settle down, to find someone to love, to be a father. His thoughts of Emma were joined by memories of Olivia. Seeing her everyday could not be a good thing.

"Hey, here comes Ava," Curt said with a hand in front of his mouth. "Why don't you hit her up for a date? I think she's got the hots for you."

Before he could say anything, Ethan saw the red hair out of the corner of his eye.

"Hey guys! What's up?"

Ethan glanced up to find a smiling Ava Pearson, tossing back her red hair, and smacking her gum. She reached out and started rubbing Ethan's shoulder.

"Where you been, sailor?" she asked, continuing to stroke him. She kept her breasts at Ethan's eye level, and the ample amount of cleavage on display was known to keep the attention of any man. Ava was well known to many of the men in the establishment, and she always had an eye for Ethan. For years, she had wanted him, every bit of him, and she was determined to wear down Ethan's defenses and let him ravish her one of these days. If only she could seduce him at the right time. She heard it through the grapevine he might have been going through some difficult things in life, and she hoped to use his vulnerability to her advantage.

"I've been real busy lately, Ava." He tried to inch out of her grasp but it was of little use. Ava liked to latch on and not let go.

"So I've heard. I've missed you." She gave him a seductive wink. "Maybe you and I could get together, have some drinks, and then talk about it all night long." She winked at him again and sunk her claws in deeper.

"Not tonight, Ava." He really wanted to say not ever, but he was too much of a gentleman.

Ava took the initiative and decided to take a seat on his thigh and wrapped her right arm around him. "Come on, Ethan. I heard Olivia's back in town." She knew all about the history between Olivia and Ethan, and given her jealousies, she didn't think Olivia was worthy of Ethan's affections. She could feel Ethan squirming underneath her, but it only caused her to sink in further into his lap. Her right breast rubbed against his chest. "How about you and I show Olivia what she missed out on by leaving you. I promise I'll be loud enough to let her hear every glorious bit of it."

Ethan caught a glimpse of Curt smirking across the table and giving him the stupid look that said Ethan should take Ava home with him and have a good time.

Ethan would have none of it. He put his hands around Ava's waist and his strong arms moved her back into a standing position next to the table. He scooted out of the booth. "I said not tonight, Ava."

She feigned shock, like she couldn't believe a red-blooded American male would rebuff her advances.

Ethan threw a five-dollar bill down on the table to cover his share of the wings and tip. "I'm not in the mood tonight, Curt. I'll see you later."

Ethan did an about-face and didn't look back. Once in his pickup, he drove slowly through the streets of Huron Cove trying to make sense of things. His mind kept going back and forth between images of Emma and Olivia. What did he want in his life? Did he want them? Or did he want to end up with someone like Ava?

He pulled to a stop outside his house. Across the lawn, he could see the lights on at the Daniels house. Olivia was probably there. And Emma was probably entertaining Bella, Olivia, and the rest of the Daniels clan in her own special way. A part of him wanted to go over there. To see Emma and Olivia and help him erase the memories of his night with Ava. He decided a night alone with his thoughts might be better.

After fixing himself a cup of coffee, he sat down at the kitchen table and opened up the manila envelope Miss White had given him when she dropped off Emma on that wild Friday night. The envelope had sat unopened since that time, its contents a mystery. He pulled out the sheets of paper stapled in the corner and read the short cover letter signed by Ashley White. He grabbed a pencil and wrote down her phone number on a pad of paper. He then flipped to the second page.

"Emma Lynn Grayson," he said out loud as he read the first box in her CPS history. There was a Polaroid picture of a beaming young girl attached with a paper clip.

"Date of birth, July third."

He gulped at the lump in his throat and looked at the

date on his digital watch. Her birthday was only five days away. In all her constant chattering, she had never mentioned when her birthday was or that she had one coming up. How sad of a thought that was. She was eight years old, and her ninth birthday could come and go without even a single notice, without a cake to blow out candles, without presents to unwrap.

He continued reading down the boxes. Parents: Deceased. Previous Guardian: Deceased. Current Guardian: Ethan Michael Stone. Siblings: None.

He was all she had in her life right now.

Ethan thought about everything he had going on between now and Emma's birthday. There would be long days ahead getting the B&B grounds into tiptop shape. The barn was almost done. Then there were the Fourth of July fireworks. Should he get a cake for her so they could celebrate—just the two of them? Or did he need to throw a party? Who would he invite? Arlene? Curt? The Daniels were the only other people he could think of. Bella, of course. What about Olivia? Would he set aside the painful memories of Olivia leaving him to let Emma enjoy her birthday? Could he?

He decided it had to be done. He'd have to call or text her or bring it up the next time he saw her. That was the right thing to do. Once that decision was made, he turned on his computer and started searching for something special for Emma.

CHAPTER 21

Ethan slept in late on Saturday morning. If eight o'clock could be considered late. But sleep eluded him much of the night. He had tossed and turned and stared at the ceiling. He couldn't stop thinking about Emma. And Olivia. Both of them together seemed to occupy his every thought, like he couldn't think of one without the other.

He ate breakfast by himself, and he was acutely aware of the silence. It was just him and his Frosted Flakes at an empty table. Just like old times. He was coming to the realization that he didn't like the silence. Or the loneliness. He liked having someone to talk to, or in Emma's case, just to listen to as she jabbered on about whatever was on her mind.

Now on their way into town, Ethan had his seatmate next to him.

"So did you and Bella have a good time last night at your sleepover?"

Emma practically bounced up and down in the front passenger seat. "Oh, yes. I had so much fun. We made a fort in the living room and played board games and watched a movie. And then Miss Olivia and Bella's mom did our hair." She shook her head to toss her new curls. Then she thrust her hands toward Ethan. "And then we painted each other's nails!"

Ethan took his eyes off the road and looked at the fluorescent pink polish. He smiled at the joy in her voice. "They look great. And your hair looks nice, too."

Emma admired her new paint job. "I had never painted my nails before. I painted Bella's nails a purple color because she likes purple. Miss Olivia went with red and Bella's mom chose light blue. Then for breakfast we had pancakes with blueberries from the Daniels' garden."

Ethan flipped on his turn signal and came to a stop. "I always loved Mrs. Daniels's blueberry pancakes."

With her sleepover report exhausted, Emma asked, "What did you do last night?"

Ethan glanced out both windows to check for traffic. He sure wasn't going to tell her the details of his night with Ava Pearson. No doubt Oprah would have something to say about that. "I just hung out with Wilfred E. Goodbear and watched the ball game."

Their first stop was at the Food Mart, and they stocked up on bread, peanut butter, strawberry jam, Frosted Flakes, chocolate milk, and a couple frozen pizzas.

"Did you know the Tigers were once owned by a guy who made a fortune selling pizza?" Emma asked as they walked through the frozen food section.

"Now that is something I did know. I met him once when I was playing ball. He sold the team to another guy who made a lot of money selling pizza. You'd have to sell a lot of pizzas to buy the Tigers today."

Emma's eyes widened when Ethan opened another freezer door. "Oh, we're getting ice cream?"

"Yep. What kind do you like?"

"Oh, I'm not very picky. I like all kinds. Chocolate, strawberry, vanilla, rocky road. They're all good."

Ethan picked out one of each and threw in a box of cones.

"Looks like we're having a party!"

Ethan wondered if his plot to surprise Emma with a birthday party had been discovered. He tried to dismiss her claim. "I just thought we'd stock up so we didn't have to come in so much."

The final tally at the checkout was about as high as Ethan could ever remember paying. "Did you say sixty-eight dollars?" he asked the young girl at the register.

"Yes, will you be using any coupons today?"

Ethan shook his head and reached for his wallet.

"Wait!" Emma said. "I have some coupons." She reached into the pocket of her shorts and pulled out a wad of paper. She started handing them to the checkout girl one at a time. "I was so excited about the ice cream I almost forgot I had some coupons for the things we bought."

The checkout girl took each scrap of paper, scanned it over the reader, and waited for the beep. There were a lot of beeps, and the more beeping the better. Ethan watched the screen as the cost of his shopping trip kept dropping.

Once she scanned the final coupon, the checkout girl looked at the screen. "So, your new total is forty-nine dollars and fifty cents."

Ethan looked at the girl and then the screen. "Wow!"

"Looks like you got yourself a pretty smart shopper there," the checkout girl said, nodding at Emma.

Ethan looked down at the beaming Emma. He could barely believe it. "Yes, I guess I do. I'm lucky to have her." He handed over the money and they packed up the cart.

After Ethan and Emma took the groceries back home and put the ice cream and pizzas in the freezer, they enjoyed a lunch of triangle PB&Js and potato chips. Once that was done, they headed back into town.

"Where are we going now?" Emma asked.

"We're going to buy you some new clothes."

Emma reached down and pulled out a handful of paper. "Can we pass out these flyers for the fireworks show while we're shopping? Miss Olivia gave me some extras."

"Sure. Are you looking forward to the fireworks?"

Emma waved her hand out the window through the passing air. "I sure am. I think they'll be beautiful with the lighthouse all lit up, too."

The pair walked into Ballantyne's Clothing Store and turned toward the girls' section. Ethan pointed at several racks of clothes. "Why don't you pick out a new shirt and some longer pants just in case it gets chilly at night."

Emma flipped through the racks, chatting as she went. "Will they have a lot of fireworks?"

Ethan looked at some of the price tags on the shirts. Not too bad, he thought. "They're usually pretty good for a small town like Huron Cove. Lots of pretty colors and big boomers."

"Have they always had a fireworks show here?"

"They have for as long as I can remember."

Emma picked out a pink shirt with white buttons down the front. "Does this look nice?" she asked, holding it up to herself.

"Yes, it does. You can try it on if you like."

Emma went to the changing room, came out and twirled around to give Ethan a look, and then went back in after finding it fit perfectly. Along with a pair of blue jeans, they went up to the checkout counter. "

"Are you going to the fireworks show?" Emma asked the young lady at the register.

"When is it?"

"It's this Saturday night," Emma said, handing over a flyer. "There's going to be food and music and lots of fun. Plus the fireworks."

The lady took the flyer and smiled. "It sounds like fun. I hope I can make it."

With a bag of clothes under his arm, Ethan held the

door open for Emma. "You're quite the saleswoman. I think she'll be there."

Emma stepped over a crack as they walked down the sidewalk toward the truck. "Can we sit with Miss Olivia during the fireworks?"

Ethan didn't respond right away. Emma's excitement over seeing the fireworks show had pushed Olivia to the back of his mind. But Emma's question brought the former love of his life right back to the forefront. Ethan and Olivia had watched at least twenty fireworks shows together, and they held hands or kissed at a dozen of them. Sometimes, after the fireworks were over, they would walk hand in hand along the shores of Lake Huron and talk about their future as a couple in love.

"Can we?"

Ethan switched the bag of clothes to his other hand. "You can sit with Olivia if you want."

Emma realized he hadn't said the three of them would sit together. She waited until they were riding down the road before she asked her next question. "Did you return the engagement ring?"

Ethan looked over at Emma and gritted his teeth. He turned his attention back to the road before he decided to pull over into a space in front of the Huron Cove Park and stopped the truck. He didn't know whether he could continue driving after a question like that.

"Where did you hear such a thing?" he asked Emma without looking at her.

"Women talk." Emma reached out and patted him on the forearm. "You don't have to tell me if you don't want to."

Ethan closed his eyes and took a deep breath. He wasn't mad at Emma. Although it brought back a flood of painful memories, he knew she just asked the question because she was curious. "Did Olivia tell you to ask me that?"

Emma shook her head. "No. Olivia wasn't in the room when Bella's mom mentioned it." She looked up at him. "It's sad to think someone would have to return an engagement ring."

"Tell me about it."

"Were you really going to ask Olivia to marry you?"

Ethan could feel the chills rippling up and down his back. He remembered it like it was yesterday. The anticipation of the day. The exhilaration of the moment. "There was no 'were' about it, Emma. I did ask her to marry me."

Emma's eyes widened. "And she said no?"

Ethan broke his trance and looked over at Emma. "Yep. She turned me down. Broke my heart into a million pieces."

"Why'd she turn you down?"

Ethan sighed. He had asked himself that question a thousand times in the last two years. When he came up with an answer, he always envisioned a picture of that smug Gerard Cologne and the Hollywood sign. "I guess she got a better offer and she took it."

Emma looked down at her folded hands on her lap. "Is that why you don't like Olivia anymore?"

Ethan rubbed the back of his neck. Is that how he came off? "It's not that I don't like her anymore. It's just that I don't want to feel the pain again." He looked her in the eye. "It hurts to have your heart broken, Emma. I hope you never have to go through that. It's something that never goes away, no matter how hard you try to forget it or erase it from your memory. It sticks with you, and every time you think of what might have been, it breaks your heart all over again."

"Why does God let people fall in love when they end up getting their hearts broken?"

Ethan looked away. "I'm not sure I know the answer to that one, Emma." After more thought, he turned his head toward her. "Maybe it helps us grow inside as people. When we find someone new after suffering heartache, we appreciate that person even more, thankful that the person accepts us for who we are—scars and all. That causes us to express our love in deeper ways and to try harder to make the relationship work."

"Even if it's the second time around?"

"Maybe."

"Do you forgive her?"

Ethan started the truck, ready to get home and forget about Olivia. "Didn't Pastor Carlton say we're all supposed to forgive?"

Emma smiled. "You were listening."

"Of course I was listening." His chest heaved with a deep sigh. "And yes, I forgive her. But, like I said, I don't want to go through it again. And I'm sure Olivia will be going away in the near future. I'm not going to let her break my heart a second time. Once is enough."

"So is that why you put the wall up between you and her?"

"The wall?"

"Yeah, the wall."

Ethan raised an eyebrow. "Is this Oprah talking again?"

"Pretty much. You're trying to keep from hurting again by putting up a wall between the two of you."

"Sounds like a smart thing to do, if you ask me."

Emma hit the button lowering the window. Enjoying the wind in her face gave her a chance to collect her thoughts. "She is truly sorry for what happened. I know that because I heard her say it. She doesn't want to break your heart again. Won't you please give her a chance to be your friend again and sit with her at the fireworks show?"

Ethan was fully prepared to tell Emma "no" but he made the mistake of glancing over at the angel looking at him. The distraction made him forget what he was going to say. "Don't look at me like that."

"Like what?"

"With those big brown eyes of yours."

Emma blinked and tilted her head just so. "But these are the eyes God gave me."

Ethan's heart melted. How could he turn down her plea that they sit with Olivia? "We'll see, Emma." While he shook his head, he somehow managed a smile to escape his lips. God, he loved this little girl. Once outside the house, he put the truck into park. "And to answer your first question. Yes. I returned the engagement ring." He then pointed a finger at her. "And you want to know the worst part? The jewelry store doesn't give you all your money back either."

CHAPTER 22

"This is going to be a fabulous place for a wedding reception!" Olivia said as she entered the barn.

The place had been completely transformed. The hardwood floors had been sanded, stained, and polished to a glassy shine. Olivia could almost see her reflection in it. The sixteen round tables were covered in white table cloths with a bouquet of flowers in the center of each one. The lighting not only highlighted the floor but also the exposed beams overhead. All eyes would be drawn up to the center ceiling and the chandelier that sparkled from every angle. Strings of white lights emanated from the chandelier to all four corners of the barn. Just like Ethan said, it looked like a mountain chalet—it just so happened to be on the shores of Lake Huron in Huron Cove, Michigan.

Olivia's eyes couldn't seem to take it all in. "Ethan, this is absolutely amazing."

Ethan stopped straightening one of the table cloths and looked around. "Thanks."

"I really mean it, Ethan. Brides are going to flip out when they see what we have to offer for the wedding receptions. It's going to be magical."

Ethan pointed toward the main door. "The way I see it, the guests will be seated with the barn doors closed. Then when the bride and groom are ready, the lights do down, the barn doors open, and the bride and groom make their grand entrance down the center to the head table."

Olivia imagined every step. "Oh, yes. With a spotlight on them the whole way."

"I can make an archway or a trestle and put it in the corner for photos." He moved around one of the tables. "Space is at a premium, of course. So when the time comes for dancing, we might have to move the tables out of the way to give everyone some more room on the dance floor."

"I really need to get a photographer in here now that it's all complete. I can just see a bride looking at our brochure or website and knowing from the moment she sees this barn that this is the place she has to have."

It had been a long time since Ethan saw the former love of his life glow with such joy. She had always had a vivacious personality—and with her radiant blonde hair, she exuded a sunny disposition. Ethan always thought of her that way—smiling, effervescent, full of life. It was no wonder she was made for the bright lights of Hollywood.

"I think you ought to consider putting yourself in the pictures as well, Olivia."

She scrunched her eyebrows at what he just said.

"A TV star offering her family's property for wedding celebrations. If brides not only see this beautiful place, but also the beauty who runs it, you'll have to turn people away."

Olivia could feel a slight blush warm her cheeks. Had Ethan Stone just called her a beauty? Was it a slip of the tongue? She couldn't remember the last time she had received a compliment like that from Ethan.

Their eyes locked on each other, a glimpse of love escaping from each of their souls. They were both seeing and feeling things both of them hadn't felt in over two years. Memories rushed back into their minds, causing their heart rates to elevate. They were once in love. Madly in love. This could have been the spot for their special day. Ethan was the first to break eye contact. Olivia bit her lip. Maybe it wasn't the right time yet. She wasn't sure what Ethan wanted. Other than to have her parents' B&B thrive, she wasn't even sure what she wanted either.

Ethan and Olivia moved out of the barn and to the beach to set up chairs for the Fourth of July. The sunny skies brought warmth to their skin as Lake Huron rippled on the shore.

Ethan had cleared the sand of a couple armfuls of driftwood and mowed several paths through the tall grass. The chairs were stacked eight high, and they would offer a place to sit for those who didn't want to stretch out on a blanket on the sand. Ethan and Olivia each started picking off one at a time.

"Where do you want 'em?" Ethan asked.

Olivia looked at the lake, the lighthouse, and the pier. "I think we ought to position them facing in between the lighthouse and the pier. That way people can get a view of both while they wait for the fireworks."

"Sounds good."

"I'm thinking about getting a photographer to take a drone video of the grounds." Olivia pointed out toward the lake. "Just imagine a video of the sunrise over Lake Huron and then a flyover of the lush green grounds and beautiful barn. Then to end it, the video would close with a shot of the lighthouse lit up at night. Oh, Ethan, it would be gorgeous. And I want it to be top notch. Like worthy of a Hollywood movie."

Ethan picked up the last chair from the stacks. "Maybe you ought to ask *Gerard*?"

Olivia stopped in midstride, as if she had run into a brick wall. She turned to look at Ethan, her mouth agape in surprise he had even mentioned Gerard's name.

Once the man's name crossed Ethan's lips, he couldn't look her in the eyes. "I'm sorry about that, Olivia. It was uncalled for, and I shouldn't have said it. You didn't deserve it."

Although he was probably right, Olivia couldn't help but feel that maybe she did deserve a stinging retort from Ethan. He had never cursed her for what she had done. He hadn't even written a sternly worded e-mail or letter telling her how she broke his heart. He kept it all inside of him all this time.

"You're not the reason I left, Ethan."

"But I wasn't reason enough for you to stay either."

Olivia looked down at the ground and tucked a strand of hair behind her ear. "Gerard treated me like dirt, Ethan. He made promises he couldn't keep, and I fell for every one of them. Once he saw I wasn't his ticket to fame and fortune, he found someone else to latch on to."

* * *

Ethan shifted his stance and didn't make eye contact. "I'm sorry to hear that." A part of him wanted to punch Gerard in the chops for treating Olivia like that, but that was a part of his life that he was trying to move on from.

Once the last chair was in place, Ethan looked over at Olivia. He still felt bad for what he said, and he thought he might be able to make amends by asking her for help. "I have a favor to ask of you."

"A favor?"

Ethan nodded. He couldn't help but remember the last time he asked her something important. It didn't go well for him. But he had to do it. He had to get beyond what happened between them in the past. He gritted his teeth and forced himself to ask. "Emma's birthday is tomorrow. I just found out about it a couple of days ago when I was going through her paperwork. I want to throw a party for her and invite some people over for cake and ice cream."

"That sounds wonderful, Ethan."

"I was wondering if you could bring Bella over. You and the rest of your family are invited as well, of course, since you all are really the only friends Emma has in Huron Cove."

She reached out and brushed him on the arm. "Of course, Ethan. We would be glad to come. Bella loves her friend, and we all love Emma, too."

Ethan noticed the touch, and the tingle it caused shot straight to the middle of his chest. *Don't open up your heart, Ethan. Olivia will be gone before long.* No matter how hard he tried, his defenses were wearing down. He couldn't help but want to hold her in his arms again. How could this be happening? He had spent the last two years walling off his feelings in an impenetrable fortress that would never be broken into again. But slowly, the chips in the walls had weakened the exterior. What had caused this?

Ethan sighed. But soon thereafter, a smile began to creep out of the corners of his mouth. From across the yard, he saw Emma of Blue Gables on her way back home.

CHAPTER 23

Ethan was able to get Emma out of the house on Saturday morning, thanks to Mrs. Daniels who suggested Emma and Bella help her put up the patriotic bunting around the porch railings for the Fourth of July. He picked up the birthday cake at the grocery store and then made a quick stop at Ballantyne's Clothing Store for one last purchase.

Once back home, he peeked out the window to make sure Emma wasn't nearby to spy on what he was doing. The cake was in the fridge, the ice cream was in the freezer, and all different kinds of pop were cooling in the ice chests. He somehow found some old wrapping paper to wrap the gifts, although he did have to use the Sunday comics for the last present. He wasn't sure whether the Daniels would buy her anything, so he made sure to wrap each gift individually to give the effect of lots of presents.

He stopped scurrying around when his phone buzzed. "Hello?"

"Hey buddy, what's up?" Curt said. "What time's the party?"

Ethan turned over his wrist. "Noon."

"Will there be adult beverages?"

Ethan grunted. "No, Curt. It's a nine-year-old's birthday party. We're having cake and ice cream. Try to be on your best behavior, will ya? This is Emma's special day."

"All right, all right, I'll behave. I'll pick up Arlene and

head out there. You want me to bring anything?"

Ethan looked around the kitchen. He thought he had everything. "Bring a couple more bags of ice, will ya? Just in case."

Checking his watch for the umpteenth time, Ethan opened the closet and pulled out a dozen helium-filled balloons in assorted colors. He tied them to the back deck and then threw a plastic tablecloth on the picnic table.

Olivia sent him a text. *Are you ready?*

His thumbs typed out a reply. *Not yet!*

Olivia responded quickly. *Do you need any help?*

Ethan looked at his watch and then tapped out a message. He didn't give a second thought about the woman he was texting. *I could use some help.*

Olivia came over in a matter of minutes. She smiled upon finding Ethan in such a harried state. He was doing his best to make this a memorable day.

"What do you need me to do?"

Ethan stopped and took a breath. In that instant, his heart skipped a beat. Olivia was in his kitchen. He couldn't help but notice her short shorts and the Michigan Wolverine T-shirt knotted at her stomach. A weird feeling came over him. He wasn't sure what it was, but it was something pleasant. Something that said being in the kitchen together was a good thing, like it was meant to be. Maybe he had dreamed it before. He shoved the thought aside. *Focus.* "Could you take the veggie tray and the plastic cups out to the deck? I'll grab the coolers."

Olivia smiled when she walked through the open sliding door and saw the deck decorated with balloons and festive plates and napkins. "Emma's going to love it, Ethan. You've done a great job." She set the tray and cups on the table. "What else?"

He surveyed the deck. He thought he had everything.

His eyes then shot toward Olivia. "Candles! I forgot candles!" He raced back into the kitchen and started opening up all the cabinets. "I can't have a birthday cake without candles."

Olivia followed him. "If you don't have any, I can see if my mom has some." She opened up a junk drawer next to the fridge. "Found 'em!"

Ethan rushed over. "How many?"

Olivia put five on the counter and rummaged around for some more. "Here's another four"

Ethan exhaled. "Thank goodness." He was nearly out of breath. *What had overcome him?*

Olivia closed the drawer and looked over at him. She reached out her hands and grabbed him by the forearms. "You've done a wonderful job, Ethan. I'm really impressed. Emma's lucky to have you in her life."

Ethan felt the touch and all he could think about was grabbing Olivia in a hug. He had the undeniable urge to hold her in his arms and never let go. They looked into each other's eyes. *What was holding him back?* The silence was broken when the screen door slammed.

"We're here!" Curt announced.

Ethan broke eye contact with Olivia and walked away. "In here." Curt and Arlene walked into the kitchen. "Everything's ready. Thanks for coming, Arlene."

Curt and Arlene were followed by Beth and Mr. Daniels and then Audrey. All that was missing was Mrs. Daniels, Bella, and the birthday girl.

* * *

"Surprise!"

A gasping Emma almost fell backwards when Mrs. Daniels brought her out to Ethan's deck and saw all the people, balloons, and gifts.

"Happy birthday, Emma!"

It was then that her emotions got the best of her and tears started cascading down her cheeks. She had never had a real birthday party before. Ethan walked up to her and bent down on one knee.

"Happy birthday, Emma. Are you okay?"

She choked back sobs. "Yes. Thank you, Mr. Ethan. I didn't even know you knew it was my birthday."

Ethan opened his arms and then wrapped them around her. Olivia was fighting back tears herself. All in attendance could tell by the way Ethan hugged Emma and closed his eyes that this little girl had touched his heart like nothing ever had before.

Olivia was next with a hug for her. "Happy birthday, Emma."

"Thank you, Miss Olivia."

Ethan escorted the birthday girl to the bench so she could be the center of attention while she opened her gifts. Emma couldn't believe the pile of wrapped presents that surrounded her.

"Smile, Emma," Olivia said, as she snapped a picture with her phone.

Unlike most nine-year-olds, Emma took her time unwrapping the gifts, as if to savor the moment as long as she could. Mr. and Mrs. Daniels got her a miniature lighthouse just like the one up the beach. It lit up when she turned it on. Bella gave her her very first Barbie doll, which she loved. Arlene brought Emma a half dozen of her world-famous triple-chocolate-chunk muffins, and she even threw in an index card containing her "secret" recipe.

"This one's from me, Emma," Olivia said, handing over the box and sitting next to her.

Ethan and Olivia moved around each other like an old married couple. He took her phone and snapped a picture of her and Emma.

Emma unwrapped the box and lifted off the lid. Inside, she found the exact same Michigan Wolverine T-shirt that Olivia was wearing as well as some of the hair care products Olivia had endorsed. Emma lifted off the tissue paper underneath those gifts to find a silver frame with a studio headshot of Olivia with the inscription: *To the beautiful Emma, Thanks for being my friend, Olivia Daniels*.

Emma grabbed the frame and clutched it to her chest. "My very own autographed picture!"

Ethan moved in next with an armful of gifts. Emma unwrapped the first one to find a Detroit Tigers T-shirt, just like his.

"Hopefully, they'll be good again before you grow out of it," he said to the laughs of others.

Sticking with the baseball theme, Ethan bought Emma a new leather glove. When they watched ball games on TV, she had mentioned she didn't think much of pink gloves. Pink gloves were for little girls. She had admired the black glove used by her favorite Tiger Jordan Foster when he patrolled centerfield, and Ethan found one at the sporting goods store just like it.

"I can't wait to play catch," she said as she popped the new glove with her fist.

That would have to wait, however, because there were still more gifts to unwrap. Another box revealed the perfect sized purse for a nine-year-old girl.

"You can put your coupons in it," Ethan said.

Emma hung it over her shoulder, and everyone pronounced it fashionable. Ethan pulled out one final box from underneath the bench.

"Here's one more, Emma." He placed it in her hands. "I hope you like it."

Emma took her time and carefully used her finger to undo the tape. She took off the paper and set it beside her. She opened the box and stared at the contents. Then she looked at Ethan and the tears of joy starting running down her cheeks again. "You bought me new books," she whispered.

Ethan smiled. "That's right. A complete set of all the *Anne of Green Gables* books, all the way up to *Anne of Ingleside*. The lady at the bookstore knew just what I wanted. She said they're very popular."

Emma put down the box of books, ran over, and threw her arms around Ethan once more. "Thank you, Mr. Ethan, thank you."

* * *

Once all the gifts were unwrapped, Olivia helped Ethan with lighting the candles on the cake. Beth's picture of Emma blowing out her candles showed Ethan and Olivia on both sides of Emma, big smiles on their faces.

Ethan cut the cake and Olivia passed out a piece to each guest. Emma sat with Bella as they discussed her new Barbie doll. Ethan took a seat next to Curt and enjoyed the cake.

Olivia sat next to Beth and Audrey, and all three took in the chattering going on around the deck. Beth leaned toward her sister. "You two make a cute couple, you know." The whisper was loud enough for Audrey to hear on the other side of Olivia.

Olivia didn't respond. She glanced at Ethan. He was laughing and smiling. He looked happy—as happy as she had ever seen him. He was the same handsome man that she had known for so many years. They were once young lovers. Back in college, she had thought he was too much of a frat boy to want to settle down. But now? The way he took to parenting Emma was something she had never seen in him before. It made her love him even more.

Would he take her back? Or had she pushed him so far away that he would never love her again? She wondered what she could do to fix things and put back the pieces of their broken relationship.

CHAPTER 24

"Did you know that Michigan has the longest freshwater shoreline in the world?" Emma said, as she and Ethan were on their way to church. "The world!"

Ethan smiled. He was glad to be going to church again and glad he had Emma along for the ride. "Wow. That's something."

"Have you ever been to the Upper Peninsula?"

Ethan thought for a second. "Just a couple of times. I think I played some baseball games up in Marquette once."

"Did you know the people in the Upper Peninsula call the rest of us 'trolls' because we live beneath the Mackinac Bridge?"

Ethan laughed. He hadn't heard that one before. "Yeah, well, those Yoopers are a weird bunch up there. Probably don't get enough sun or something."

After entering the church sanctuary, Ethan and Emma took the back row—Emma having decreed that to be "their spot," at least until she could twist Ethan's arm to sit with the Daniels family—and they settled in. The five minutes that remained prior to the start of the service gave Emma time to talk.

"Will we have time to pick cherries today?" she asked Ethan.

"Sure. We'll go out to the orchard right after the service. The cherries should be ready. I don't know whether the apricots will be ready or not."

"When will the apples be ready? I love apples."

"Apples and pears usually get ripe for picking in September and October. It looks like we're going to have a good crop this year."

"Can we make applesauce?"

For a split second, Ethan caught himself. A few weeks ago, he wanted nothing more than to send Emma Lynn Grayson on her way to live with a good family who would love and take care of her. That way he could go back to living his normal life. If a question about making applesauce in the fall would have been asked, he would have thought she wouldn't be around long enough to find out. She'd be long gone from Huron Cove and simply a memory from a wild couple of weeks. But those thoughts had been pushed to the back of his mind. He wanted her here. And he wanted Emma to be there with him in the fall so they could pick apples and make applesauce. He had come to realize that he loved her and wanted her to be a permanent part of his life.

"Sure, we can make applesauce."

"Well, hello there, little angel," Arlene said. She took a seat next to Emma. "How are you now that you've turned nine years old?"

Emma smiled. "It feels the same as when I was eight. Thanks for the muffins and the recipe. I hope to make them someday." She glanced over at Ethan and then back at Arlene. "But first, we'd have to buy the mix . . . and the eggs and the oil and the muffin pan."

Arlene laughed. "You mean Ethan doesn't have all that in his kitchen already?"

Emma smirked and shook her head. Her eyes were then drawn to the blonde hair walking down the right side of the church. She tapped Ethan on the thigh and leaned closer to him. "There's Olivia. Doesn't she look beautiful today?"

Ethan didn't need to have Olivia pointed out to him or questioned about her beauty. He had spotted her as soon as she made her way down toward the front of the church. She looked particularly radiant today. The dress was a brilliant red, the color that Ethan always found most attractive with her long blonde hair.

Try as he might, he couldn't stop thinking about being with her. He wanted to sit next to her, interlock his fingers with hers, and never let go. He could think of nothing better than to spend his Sundays in church with Olivia Daniels. His breathing slowed, and he closed his eyes.

"Did you hear me?"

Ethan opened his eyes and nodded. *Sundays in church with Olivia Daniels—and Emma, too.* "Yeah. She does look beautiful today."

At the conclusion of the service, Pastor Carlton left the parishioners with a final thought. "I hope you all have a blessed week and a happy Fourth of July. As we head out for our busy summer vacations and Independence Day celebrations, let us remember the words of Saint Paul in Ephesians, chapter four, verse two: 'Be completely humble and gentle; be patient, bearing with one another in love.'"

* * *

With the Fourth of July festivities on the lake not set to begin until five o'clock, Ethan had Curt and a couple of buddies over beforehand to watch the Tigers on TV. They planned to make a day of it and then head out to the beach to help Olivia put on the finishing touches before the crowd started to show up for the music and the fireworks.

Cory Anderson played baseball with Ethan at Michigan before becoming a police officer in Bay City. Alex Armstrong had known Ethan and Curt since their days at Huron Cove High. He worked construction up and down the Sunrise Coast. Cory and Alex were always welcome at Ethan's bachelor pad, although the bawdy jokes and freewheeling conversation had been toned down given a certain female currently flitting about in the house.

Curt had plopped himself down in the recliner and lamented the sorry state of the Tigers team this year. "I can't remember when the Tigers played so poorly on defense." He raised his can of cola to his mouth and drained it to the bottom.

Cory Anderson agreed. "It's not like it used to be. Fundamentals have taken a back seat to the long ball. It's all about the home run now."

Emma spent the good part of the first two innings scurrying back and forth from the living room to the kitchen. With her oversized apron tucked underneath and tied twice around, she answered every request for more chips, salsa, and napkins. Plus, she did it all with a smile and gracious attitude because she wanted to impress Ethan in front of his friends.

Ethan was taking notice. But there was something else about it. He expected nothing more from Emma. She wasn't one to whine and moan about work. She liked feeling wanted, even if it was just a couple of guys she didn't know. Ethan, however, was focused more on his buddies. He would have been like them just a short time ago. They were all single, focused on having a good time, and certainly not caregivers to nine-year-old girls. But Ethan was, and he realized he needed to start acting like it.

Alex took a moment during a commercial to talk gossip with the guys. He looked over at Ethan. "I heard you and Olivia are back together."

Ethan looked at Curt and frowned. He must have been feeding the guys bad information just to yank his chain. "We're not back together. I've just been doing some work over at the Daniels' B and B and helping Olivia get ready for the fireworks show."

Cory knew Olivia from when she and Ethan were an item at the University of Michigan. "Curt says she's still looking pretty good."

"I don't want to talk about her, guys."

Curt leaned toward Ethan and tried to stir the pot some more. "You know, you're going to need a mother for that girl someday."

Ethan could almost sense Emma eavesdropping behind the kitchen door, her ears probably straining to hear what he had to say in response.

"Yeah, I know."

"Have you thought of that?"

The three guys sat looking at Ethan, oblivious to the fact the game had resumed in the top of the third. No one was watching the TV.

Ethan was looking out the window toward the Daniels' house. "Of course, I've thought about it." He knew full well Emma was going to need a mother in her life. But who would it be? Ethan didn't know. Only God knew right now. "I just haven't figured it all out yet. I'm sure God will steer me in the right direction, wherever that may take me."

Curt grinned broadly. "I bet Ava might be interested. I'm not sure what kind of a mother she'd be, but I bet you'd be taken care of just right." He threw in a wink in case Ethan wasn't getting the message.

"Hey, Emma," Cory said, raising his empty cola can in the air as she came back into the living room. "Get me another cold one from the fridge, will ya, please?"

Emma nodded. "Yes, sir." She did an about-face and headed for the kitchen.

"Yeah, get one for me, too, Toots," Curt said, giving

her a playful tap on the fanny to hurry her along.

Ethan's eyes widened and his jaw clenched as he took in the scene. Emma might not have a woman to call a mother in her life at the present time, but there was a guy who could act like her father. He turned his head toward the kitchen. "Emma, come here. Right now."

Emma stuck her head back into the living room without the drinks. "Yes?"

"Come here." Ethan patted the open spot on the couch next to him. "Sit down. You're going to sit down and watch the ball game with me." He again motioned her to the couch. "Sit down."

She sat in the middle of the couch and stared at the floor, her hands folded in her lap. She thought she had done something wrong.

"Stay right here." Ethan got up, walked over to Curt in the recliner, and wagged a finger in his face. "Her name is not Toots."

Ethan walked into the kitchen, opened up the fridge, and grabbed a can of cola. On his way back to the living room, he shook the can a dozen times and then handed it to Curt. "Don't ever call her that again."

"I'm sorry, I'm sorry. You know I'm joking around. I just thought it would be nice to have a servant like you do." Curt popped the top and the cola spray hit him all over. "Aw, man," he said, as he sat up and the splattered liquid rolled down his face.

Somehow Emma kept from smiling, but Ethan's smirk was clear as day. "She's not my servant, Curt," he announced proudly, putting his arm around her shoulders and pulling her close. "She's my daughter."

CHAPTER 25

Despite the Tigers making a late-inning comeback with a pair of three-run homers, Ethan turned off the TV a little after five. The guys had already left to pick up their dates for the Fourth of July extravaganza on the lake, and Ethan could tell Emma was itching to head to the beach to see how the preparations were going. Of course, asking "Is it time?" every five minutes was a good indicator she was not that interested in the outcome of the ball game.

"Are you excited?" Ethan asked as they walked out the back door.

"Oh, yes. I could just burst." Emma wore a new pair of jean shorts and a red-white-and-blue T-shirt that Mrs. Daniels bought for her. Bella had the exact same shirt, and they were both going to wear them to the celebration. "There's going to be so much to take in."

Ethan laughed. "Well, you've got lots of time. It's supposed to run from six until the fireworks are over. So, pace yourself."

"Okay." As they neared the beach, Emma looked up at Ethan. In all the excitement that was on the agenda, she felt the need to say something. "Thank you, Mr. Ethan."

"For what?"

"For being so good to me. For the last couple of weeks, I haven't even thought about being an orphan or without a real home. It's nice to have someone care about me."

Ethan put his arm around her shoulder. "It's been my pleasure, Emma. I'll always care about you." As soon as they hit the beach, they saw Bella waving from near the Daniels' house. "There's Bella. Looks like she's ready for some fun, too."

Emma grabbed his hand. "Come on!"

They met up with Audrey and Bella and all of them stopped to look out over the beach.

"It's going to be a beautiful evening for the celebration," Audrey said.

Two-hundred white chairs sat neatly on the beach ready for attendees, and there was plenty of sand for those who brought their own or would make do with a blanket. The Huron Cove High School marching band members were setting up their instruments on the pier and beginning to warm up before the show began. The barge on the lake was anchored in place and the firework tubes were ready for liftoff. A few boaters were already staking out their spot.

To go along with the hot dogs ready for the grill and the buns sitting on the table, Mr. Butler from the Food Mart could be seen carrying aluminum-foil pans full of baked beans and potato salad to the concession area. Buckets of ice kept cans of pop cool for those in need of refreshment. Everything was ready for the citizens of Huron Cove looking to celebrate Independence Day.

Ethan's eyes searched up and down the beach for the one citizen who put the whole thing together. He then turned toward Audrey. "Where's your sister?"

"Olivia? She's around here somewhere. I saw her running around trying to get everything ready earlier." Audrey looked back toward the Daniels' house and saw her. "There she is. She must have had to change her clothes."

Ethan's heart skipped a beat when he saw Olivia walking through the gate onto the beach. Her hundred-dollar jean shorts did little to hide her tanned and toned legs. Her red-and-blue button-down shirt with white stars captured the spirit of the holiday. Everything about her told everyone she was the All-American girl.

"Hi, Miss Olivia!" Emma said, running over to give her a hug.

"Oh, thanks for coming, Emma." Olivia gave her an extra long squeeze. "I love your shirt. You look so festive."

Maybe it was the warm evening or the celebratory mood of those in attendance, but Ethan could feel his heart pounding in his chest. Seeing Olivia with Emma, both of them happy, made him want to see more of it. Why did he keep trying to bury those feelings? Why couldn't he tell Olivia how he truly felt? That he wanted her in his life. Correction—that he wanted her in his life *and* Emma's life.

Emma directed Olivia's attention to Ethan. "Doesn't Mr. Ethan look handsome tonight?"

Olivia's gaze turned toward her friend of so many years. She took in how his white T-shirt wrapped around his muscular chest and chiseled arms. Filling out the jeans the way he did, she couldn't help but think how he had turned into a man.

"Yes, he is looking handsome tonight." Olivia walked over and gave Ethan a hug. "Thanks for coming," she said softly in his ear. "And thanks for all your help with setting up."

Ethan could smell the strawberries in her hair, and he desperately wanted to wrap his arms around her. It was almost like the fireworks display had started early, and he hoped she couldn't feel the pounding of his heart through his chest. He managed to give her a couple of pats on the back.

Was he falling in love with Olivia Daniels again? Was it going to work out this time? He realized he wanted it to. His heart told him to take the chance once again, to love her like he always had.

"I just wanted to say . . ." Ethan's sentence was cut short by the man at the microphone asking all those in attendance to rise for the national anthem. What Ethan had to say would have to wait.

* * *

Emma was thoroughly enjoying herself. She and Bella twirled sparklers in the air. Emma loved the patriotic music and eating hot dogs. She also liked seeing all the people having a good time. But there were two people that weren't enjoying themselves as much as she wanted them to. No matter how hard she tried, she couldn't get Ethan and Olivia to share a quiet moment between them. Something had to be done.

"Emma, are you having a good time?" Ethan asked, sitting down on the large blanket he had grabbed from the house.

"Yes, I am, thank you. There are a lot of people here."

Ethan nodded. "More than I expected, and that's good. It's good to see the community come out and enjoy themselves."

"Are you having a good time?" Emma asked.

Ethan looked over at her. "Yeah. It's nice to see some old friends and familiar faces."

Emma tried to steer the conversation in her intended direction. "Doesn't Olivia look beautiful tonight?"

Ethan cast his gaze on Olivia. As the sun set, the yellow, orange, and red hues caught Olivia in all the right places. With the darkening backdrop to the east over Lake Huron, her golden hair and tanned face radiated in the last light of the day.

Ethan couldn't lie about it. "Yes, she does look beautiful tonight."

Emma looked over at Ethan. She could tell there was still love in his heart for Olivia. But there was something holding him back. Something that wouldn't let him drop his guard and let Olivia back into his life.

Emma felt like she couldn't wait any longer. She was going to have to bring them together any way she could. "Olivia! Olivia! Over here!"

She finally got Olivia's attention, and her waving hand directed Olivia to the blanket she shared with Ethan. Emma scooted toward the edge and patted the spot between her and Ethan.

"Would you like to sit down?"

Olivia took a seat in between them and gave a quick sigh like she was glad to get off her feet for a few minutes. "Are you having a good time, Emma?"

"Oh, yes. I'm so excited for the fireworks. I've never been to a real live fireworks show."

Olivia smiled. "Where's Bella?"

"She went back to the house to use the bathroom. She'll be back in a little bit."

A nearby bonfire roared to life, and Emma could see the flames flickering in Olivia's eyes. Emma looked over at Ethan. "Didn't Olivia do a great job putting this all together, Mr. Ethan?"

Ethan had barely taken his eyes off Olivia ever since she sat down. She was incredibly beautiful, and maybe even more talented. She was the reason everything came together. He spoke directly to her. "You really did a great job, Olivia. I'm impressed with everything—the music, the food, finding a place for people to enjoy themselves."

Olivia smiled and gave him a wink. "I had good people

helping me."

"The Fourth of July in Huron Cove wouldn't have been the same without fireworks, and you're the reason all these people are here."

Emma suddenly felt the need to leave Olivia and Ethan alone. This was what she had been hoping for. Before she could scamper off the blanket, someone decided to throw a wrench into her plans.

"Olivia Daniels!" the woman exclaimed.

Olivia instantly recognized Tracie Bonner, her former cheerleading coach from high school, and her husband Carl. She jumped up off the blanket to greet them. "It's so nice to see you," she said, giving Tracie a hug.

"Oh, we were hoping to see you here tonight. We heard you were back in town and putting this all together." She turned to look at the assembled crowd. "You've done a great job."

"Thank you."

"And it's such a wonderful setting, too."

Olivia couldn't agree more. "I bet all the creators in Hollywood couldn't recreate a more beautiful spot than right here in Huron Cove, Michigan."

Carl Bonner interjected. "Speaking of Hollywood—when are we going to see you on TV again?" His wife looked on with great anticipation.

Although Olivia couldn't give a definitive answer, the Bonners didn't care. They gushed over their famous acquaintance.

"We're so proud of you," Tracie said. "We just know, one day, you're going to win an Academy Award or an Emmy or something." She looked down at Ethan and handed him her phone. "Would you take a picture of us?"

Emma watched as Ethan slowly got off the blanket. He looked at the trio in the phone's screen and tapped the button. As soon as he was done, he had another request for his photography services. Like moths to a light, people flocked to be around Olivia, and everyone wanted a piece of Huron Cove's TV star. She was soon dragged away to say hello to another fawning admirer.

Emma looked up at Ethan, who stood there in silence. The whirlwind that was Olivia Daniels had blown through, and Ethan acted like he was just another piece of wreckage left behind. Emma started to get up from the blanket, wanting to take hold of Ethan's hand. Something to take his mind off Olivia. Emma could tell Ethan thought Olivia could never be anything other than the center of attention, and that center would forever be linked to Hollywood and her acting career.

"Emma, do you want another bottle of water?" The tone of his voice indicated he had resigned himself to the fact that Olivia would never be a part of his life.

"No, thank you, Mr. Ethan." Before she could go to him, Bella came rushing back and grabbed her hand. She had somewhere that they needed to be.

After Bella introduced Emma to her Sunday School pals, Emma looked back to the blanket. The fireworks would start in half an hour, but Ethan wasn't there. She hoped he hadn't gone back home. Her gaze finally found him standing near the water line—alone with his thoughts. He was looking east over the darkened lake. She could tell his heart was breaking. She had wanted Ethan and Olivia to get together tonight, and she thought Ethan wanted the same. Then they could all be together. All three of them. Just like a family.

She decided she only had one more opportunity, and she was determined to make it count. She grabbed her friend's hand. "Come on, Bella, let's get our spot for the fireworks."

* * *

The fireworks were a huge hit. The Huron Cove City Council had found a little more in the coffers to make it a show everyone would remember, and no one in attendance would leave disappointed. All colors of the rainbow lit up the night sky and reflected off the shimmering water of Lake Huron. With every bright flash of white, a silhouette of the lighthouse reminded everyone why they loved living in Huron Cove.

Once the grand finale had ended and the crescendo of the music subsided, the master of ceremonies took to his microphone one last time.

"Thank you, ladies and gentlemen, for attending the Fourth of July spectacular on the lake. We do hope you had a good time. Please drive home safely."

Ethan had drifted farther down the beach. He saw some of the fireworks, but his eyes were drawn more toward the sand. His head shook with every other thought. He had hoped tonight would be a new beginning in a relationship with Olivia. He had begun to see her as a mother to Emma. He had even let himself dream of the three of them becoming a family. He tried to shake the thought out of his head. It was never going to happen. He was going to have to come to grips with that fact. She was a Hollywood star, and Huron Cove was just a stopping point for her until the star took off once again. His head finally nodded in agreement. It had become apparent that God's plan for Ethan didn't include Olivia Daniels, and he was going to have to make the best of it—for his sake and for Emma's. He took a deep cleansing breath and felt at peace with himself. If his life had nothing more than Emma, then it would have purpose. He turned and looked for Emma at the blanket but didn't see her.

As the crowd began to head home, Ethan started

walking back up the beach. He thought he and Emma might enjoy a piece of leftover birthday cake and a bowl of ice cream before calling it an evening. He stopped, wondering where she was.

Ethan took a slow look toward the pier, and then the lighthouse, and then to the Daniels' B&B, and then finally over to his house. He then did it again faster in reverse order. He felt a twinge in his gut. He started looking for someone he knew. Anyone who might know Emma.

He continued looking around, his eyes squinting into the beams of headlights and peering through the darkness over the lake. *Could she have gone into the water? He didn't even know whether she could swim. What if someone had kidnapped her? He hadn't even taught her about "stranger danger."* All sorts of terrible thoughts filled his mind.

Ethan's heart was racing, and he could feel a tightness in his throat. He tried not to think it. *What if he lost Emma forever?*

He started walking back to the blanket where he had last seen her. With still no sign of her, he picked up the pace. Upon catching a glimpse of blonde hair in the light of the bonfire, his head snapped toward Olivia. He sprinted toward her, his shoes churning through the sand, and grabbed her by the arm.

"Have you seen Emma?"

CHAPTER 26

"No, I haven't seen her in a while." She was shocked by the concern in his wide eyes. "Ethan, what's wrong?"

Ethan continued to look in every direction. A cool breeze off the lake hit him in the face. It would only get colder. "I can't find her. I don't know where she is."

Olivia reached out and touched him on his forearm. "Maybe she got tired and went back to your house," she said, trying to sound reassuring.

Ethan quickly dismissed it. "Emma had her heart set on seeing the fireworks. That's all she had been talking about for the last week. She wouldn't have missed them."

Olivia looked around. "I don't see Bella either."

"Emma!" Ethan yelled. He used his hands as a megaphone. "Emma!"

"I don't see them, Ethan. Why don't you go check at your place and I'll go see if they're at my mom and dad's."

Ethan took off running for his house, his gut twisting into tighter knots the closer he got. He took the steps two at a time and hit the porch.

"Emma?"

The front door was unlocked, just like it always was. The lamp was on in the living room. Did he leave it on?

He yelled louder this time. "Emma? Are you in here?"

He bounded up the steps and threw open the door to her room. The bed was made, and Wilfred E. Goodbear sat against the headboard. He checked her closet just in case. He ran into his room and searched any space big enough to hide her. He looked in her bathroom, the hall closet, and the third bedroom. He stopped to think. His chest heaved up and down as he tried to catch his breath. *Where could she be?*

"Emma?"

He ran back downstairs and into the garage. He checked inside his truck and the bed in the back. Empty. *Emma, where are you?* He forced his mind to come up with an answer. *Where would Anne of Green Gables go?* Somehow he remembered Emma mentioning something about a haunted woods in the book. He gasped at the answer. *The orchard!*

Ethan ran into the darkness of the trees, the smell of apples filling his nostrils.

"Emma!"

He heard his voice die amongst the leafy branches as he passed row after row of trees.

"Emma? Are you in here?"

He heard nothing but the squishing of last year's fallen apples under his shoes. She wasn't in there. He turned and sprinted toward the light of the Daniels' house. Olivia was walking toward him. *Had she found them?* His heart filled with relief and hope.

But that hope drained from his body when he saw Olivia shake her head and hold out her hands. "Ethan! Did you find them?"

Ethan shook his head. He met up with Olivia, and he could see the worry in her eyes.

"My parents said they haven't seen Bella or Emma since before the fireworks started."

Ethan ran a hand through his hair. "I don't know where they are."

Both of them continued looking in every direction. Olivia tried to take a breath. "Okay, let's think this through, Ethan. Emma doesn't know anybody other than my family, does she?"

Ethan's trembling hand wiped a cold layer of sweat off his forehead. "Uh . . . um . . . There's Curt and the guys. And she knows Arlene, of course. Maybe Pastor Carlton, but that's about it."

Olivia reached out and patted Ethan on the arm. "Why don't you call or text Curt and Arlene. Maybe they saw her."

Ethan's texts were quickly returned. Curt and Arlene didn't know where Emma was. *Nobody knew where Emma was!*

Ethan's eyes met Olivia's. He could barely stammer out the words. "I don't know what to do, Olivia. Maybe we should call the police."

Olivia stepped closer to him and grabbed his arms. "Ethan, look at me." She gave him a quick shake. "Look at me, Ethan. It's going to be okay. We're going to find her, you and me."

Ethan gulped and focused on what Olivia was saying. "What about your sisters and parents?"

"I told them Bella might have been over at your house. I'll run back there and tell them we need them to help look."

Ethan looked out toward the dark waters of Lake Huron. "I'm going to go check the pier."

Before he took off, Olivia squeezed his arms tighter. "It's gonna be okay, Ethan. We're gonna find them."

Ethan's shoes thumped heavy on the planks of the pier. Once he reached the end, he looked out over the lake.

"Emma? Bella?"

He leaned over the railing and saw nothing but the black depths of Lake Huron.

Please God, don't let them be in the water.

The light from the lighthouse skimmed across the rippling water, and Ethan followed the shine from the north shore to the south. The boaters had left, and the only sound was the water lapping against the pier pylons.

Ethan's concentration was broken when he heard voices in the distance.

"Emma! Bella!"

Olivia's parents and sisters had joined the search party. Ethan ran back toward them and met up with Olivia.

"They're not at the pier. I didn't see anyone in the water."

Olivia took a breath. She looked at Ethan and then watched the light from above search the water below. She turned her head north. "Have you checked the lighthouse?"

Ethan looked toward the lighthouse, its beacon of light piercing the darkness with every pass. *It was the only place they hadn't looked. It was their last hope.* "Let's go."

They made it to the rocky shoreline surrounding the lighthouse and looked at every crevice. It would have been so easy to have slipped on a rock and fallen into the water. Ethan didn't want to think it, but he jumped into the knee-deep water and splashed around the perimeter.

"Emma? Bella?" His voice was growing hoarse, and each shout of her name had a tinge more anguish in it. He couldn't lose her. *Please God, don't take her from me.*

He made it around to the north side.

"Anything?" Olivia asked.

Ethan shook his head. "Nothing."

Olivia looked up and watched the light spin around. She pointed up at the lighthouse. "Ethan, do you think she would have gone up to the top?"

Ethan grabbed hold of the rocks and pulled himself out of the lake. He met Olivia at the door, and then he tried the knob. It was unlocked. He turned it, yanked open the door, and yelled up the spiral staircase with every last bit of strength he had.

"Emma! Bella!"

CHAPTER 27

"Emma! Bella! Are you up there?"

Ethan took the stairs two at a time. This was the last place on earth he hadn't looked. If she wasn't here, he would have to do the last thing a parent ever wanted to do. Call the police to report missing children.

Please Lord, let me find them.

Halfway up, he thought he heard something. He lightened his footfalls and strained to listen for the sound again. He stopped and looked behind him at Olivia. "Did you hear that?"

They both listened in silence.

"Emma? Bella?"

He heard the sound again. The muffled thud of someone banging on a door. Then there was something else. Ethan cocked his head toward the top of the lighthouse to hear better.

"Mr. Ethan!"

"Emma!" Ethan yelled. He bounded up the stairs again. "I'm coming, Emma!"

Nearly out of breath, Ethan and Olivia made it up the staircase to a landing leading to a steel door.

"Mr. Ethan!" Emma pounded her fist against the door again.

"We're here, Emma!" For a moment, Ethan relaxed. He had found her. *Thank God!* He looked at Olivia and then back at the door. "Emma, is Bella with you?"

"Yes, she's right here. We can't open the door."

Olivia reached out and clasped Ethan's arm. She finally took a breath and thanked the Lord.

Ethan could hear Emma yanking on the door handle, but her nine-year-old strength was no match for the heavy metal door.

"Stand back from the door, Emma. You and Bella go up the stairs to the lantern room and wait, okay?"

"Okay."

Ethan waited for a second, braced himself, and then pounded the door with the sole of his right shoe. The door moved an inch but wouldn't budge. Ethan drove his shoulder into it and the door flew open. He looked up the stairs and found what he had been looking for. Finally.

"Mr. Ethan!"

She jumped down the stairs and into his arms. Bella was enveloped by her Aunt Olivia.

Ethan didn't know whether Emma was trembling or if it was him. All he knew was, he was glad to have Emma back safe and sound. He released her from his hug but held onto her arms and looked into her eyes. "Emma, what are you two doing up here?"

For once in her life, Emma struggled to find the right words. "I . . . I . . . we wanted to watch the fireworks. . . and I thought it would be cool to watch them from up in the lighthouse. But once they were over, we couldn't get back down because the door was stuck."

Ethan found the explanation plausible. She had her heart set on seeing the fireworks, and getting the best view was important. "But why didn't you tell us where you and Bella were going to be, Emma?"

"I'm sorry, Mr. Ethan." Tears pooled in her eyes. "I couldn't find you, and I knew the fireworks were starting soon. I just grabbed Bella and told her to follow me. I'm really sorry."

"I'm sorry, too, Aunt Olivia," Bella cried. She was starting to shiver in the cold darkness of the lighthouse.

Ethan gave Emma another hug, and Olivia did the same with Bella.

"Come on, let's get you home, Bella," Olivia said, grabbing her niece's hand. "Your mom is probably worried sick."

A cool breeze off the lake met them when they stepped out of the lighthouse. All of the locals who had attended the fireworks show had gone home, and the only voices heard were from the Daniels' search party.

"Bella?" came from off in the distance.

Olivia saw her sister and waved her hand. "Over here! We found her! They were stuck up in the lighthouse."

Audrey rushed over to them and grabbed Bella in a hug. "What were you doing up there?"

"I . . . we wanted to watch the fireworks."

Audrey grabbed her by the hand. "Don't you ever do that again."

Emma searched for some moisture in her mouth to speak. "It's my fault, Miss Audrey. I was the one who wanted to go up in the lighthouse. It wasn't Bella's fault."

Audrey reached out and touched Emma on the shoulder. She understood, but still. Mother and daughter would have a good conversation in the future. That was for sure. "It's okay. I'm just glad everyone's all right." She looked up at Olivia. "I'm going to get Bella back home."

Audrey and Bella left for the Daniels' house, and for the first time in a long time, Ethan and Olivia had a chance to look at each other. Both of them sighed in relief at the ordeal. Thankful that it was over.

"I better get Emma back home, too," Ethan said. He held out his hand toward Emma. She took hold with her left hand.

Before Olivia could respond, Emma reached out to Olivia with her right hand.

Olivia couldn't really decline the silent offer. "I'll walk with you two."

* * *

"I'm really sorry, Mr. Ethan," Emma said quietly, as the three walked along the beach.

"It's okay, Emma. We'll talk more about this tomorrow. We've had a long day, and it's time for you to go to bed and get some sleep."

Emma Lynn Grayson was not stupid. She was also not prone to doing things that would put herself or others in harm's way. She was highly intelligent for her age, and she knew all about stranger danger and the need to tell adults where she was going to be so as not to get lost. She had anticipated a stern talking to from Ethan. That's what he was supposed to do as her guardian. She would have expected nothing less. If she could have remembered them, her parents would have scolded her for wandering off without telling anybody. Aunt Millie and Uncle Charlie would have done the same. So there were no tears in her eyes for being in the wrong.

But there was something else about her. Something that told her she had to leave her comfort zone and go against all of the safety lessons she had been taught. Sometimes she had to do things she wouldn't normally do.

How else could she bring together two people destined for each other?

Of course, she should have told Ethan that she and Bella were going to watch the fireworks from the lighthouse. But he might have told her that people weren't allowed inside at night. Or maybe he would have told her to watch the fireworks with him—just the two of them on the blanket on the beach.

Or maybe she could have left the lighthouse's metal door open so she and Bella could walk back down once the fireworks were over. But then what? Would she find Ethan alone ready to go home? What good would that do? No good at all, that's what. She'd be right back at square one.

But now?

With her left hand in Ethan's and her right hand in Olivia's, they walked back toward Ethan's house—her home, and maybe one day it could be *their* home. Her heart warmed with the thought of the people holding her hands. She was the bridge between them. Unseen by Ethan and Olivia, the slightest smile crept out of the corner of Emma's mouth.

CHAPTER 28

Ethan waited until Emma returned from the bathroom with her *I'm not tipsy, I'm from Ypsi* nightshirt and then tucked her into bed. For a minute, he thought about what a real father would say to her. *You're grounded, young lady! No TV for a week!* Something that would grab her attention and let her know he meant business. But for some reason, the fatherly lecture didn't come. He couldn't bring himself to yell at her or even mildly scold her. Not now. Not with the sweet little brown-eyed girl with Wilfred E. Goodbear in her arms looking up at him. He was too exhausted. Too busy thanking God for bringing her back safe and sound.

"Good night, Emma."

"Good night, Mr. Ethan."

He left the bedroom door ajar and stepped softly down the stairs. He opened the front screen door and found Olivia sitting on the front porch swing. He didn't hesitate to sit down next to her.

"Is Emma okay?"

Ethan blew out a breath and smiled. "She's fine. I think she'll probably be asleep in no time. All the excitement wore her out."

For a couple of minutes, Ethan and Olivia sat in silence, listening only to the creaking of the rusty chain as they swung back and forth. Ethan could feel Olivia stealing glances at him, and he was pretty sure she could feel him doing the same at her.

Olivia broke the silence first. "I'm glad to hear that *Emma*'s okay, but what about *you*?"

Ethan turned his head, his eyes meeting Olivia's. He saw the light from the living room hit the side of her cheek and reflect off her golden blonde hair. He wondered if she caught him catch his breath. He took a breath to try to calm himself. He turned his eyes toward the lake.

"I think I'm okay." He flexed his hands to release some of the tension that had built up over the last hour. "I probably won't sleep a lot tonight." He looked Olivia in the eye. "It's the first time anything like that has ever happened to me. It's not like my dog ran away or anything like that. It was Emma. I thought I might have lost her. I kept thinking about her being kidnapped or falling into the lake. I don't know what I would've done if something happened to her."

"You really love her, don't you?"

Ethan nodded. "Like she's my very own daughter." He then shook his head, struggling to find the right words for the moment. A couple weeks ago, he had nothing in his life. Now he had a girl upstairs that meant the world to him. *How does something like that happen? I'm not her father.* "I don't know where it all came from."

"You mean the love you have for her?"

"Yeah."

"I think it's always been there, Ethan. Deep down inside you. You've always had a big heart. I know that firsthand. You're all she has in this world right now, and you would do everything to keep her safe."

When she reached over and grabbed his hand, it sent a jolt through his body. He felt it from his head to his toes. She was the only one in the world who could cause that feeling. He closed his eyes, his heart rate rising. She scooted close, and for the first time in what seemed like forever, Ethan had Olivia's body against his. It was like they never left, like their lives had never parted. They sat on the gently rocking swing. The silence between them spoke volumes. They didn't need to say anything because it felt so right to each of them. They were both where they wanted to be. He inhaled deeply, and he could smell the strawberry scent from Olivia's hair. So many memories swirled around in his head. A feeling of peace washed over him, like nothing else beyond this comfortable white house in Huron Cove, Michigan, mattered.

She didn't let go of his hand, and he had no desire to take it away. He could feel the wall starting to crumble. And he wanted it to crumble—every last bit of brick and masonry that he had put up between them. He wanted to break through, tear it down, and never let go of her. He opened his eyes and turned toward her.

"Thanks for being there for me tonight, Olivia. I don't know if I could have gotten through it without you."

Olivia gripped his hand harder. "I'm glad I was here for you, Ethan. And I hope you'll give me the chance to be there for you in the future."

* * *

In the house behind them, Olivia and Ethan had no clue that a nine-year-old girl had slipped out of bed and tiptoed down the hall. She had left Wilfred E. Goodbear back in the bedroom, and now she sat in the shadows at the top of the stairs. *What a night it had been.* She pulled her nightshirt over her knees and leaned forward to get a better view. Through the big picture window, she could see Olivia and Ethan sitting on the porch swing. Their words went unheard, but that was okay. Emma knew they were talking about her. They looked like they were smiling at each other. When Olivia leaned over and kissed Ethan on the cheek, Emma closed her eyes and smiled.

Thank you Lord.

Then, she went back to bed.

CHAPTER 29

Ethan was surprised to not find Emma waiting for him in her room like usual. The bed had been made, and Wilfred E. Goodbear had taken his usual spot against the headboard for the day. *Had she run away?* Goodness, he didn't want to go through that again. The clanking of dishes from the kitchen let Ethan know that he didn't need to send out another search party.

He tiptoed down the stairs and inched forward. He peeked around the refrigerator and saw the breakfast table was set. Bowls of cereal were ready, and Ethan could smell a pan of Mrs. Daniels's cinnamon rolls warming in the oven. He leaned his head forward just enough to catch a glimpse of Emma on a step stool at the sink. Her apron was fastened tight. Yellow rubber gloves covered her arms up to her elbows, and she attacked the dishes like a seasoned professional—scrubbing, rinsing, then drying. More chipper than usual, she hummed an energetic tune and danced in place as she worked.

Ethan backed up into the living room and then loudly cleared his throat to announce his presence. "Good morning, Emma."

With her hands full of pans and suds, she could only turn her head slightly. "Good morning, Mr. Ethan."

He stood next to her and held out his hand for the clean pot. "Here, let me help you there." He grabbed a towel and wiped the pot dry. He noticed she was still bouncing and swaying to the tune playing in her head. "How'd you sleep?"

"Very well, thank you." She handed him another pot. "I'm really sorry again about last night."

Ethan put the pot in the cupboard. "That's okay." He cleared his throat. *Maybe now was a time to try out that father thing.* "Just remember to tell us where you're going next time. We were looking all over for you, and it gave us quite a scare."

"Yes, sir. I'll be sure to do that." She handed over a clean plate. "Did you and Olivia have a nice talk last night?"

Ethan noticed how quickly she moved on to the next subject. Something was up. He wiped the plate dry with the towel. "What makes you think Olivia and I talked last night?"

Emma flinched and dropped the plate into the sudsy water. She hurried to grab it and rinse it off. "Um . . . I just thought I heard you go outside after I went to bed. And since Olivia walked over with us, I thought you might have walked her back home. Maybe you two talked or something."

That Emma was grasping at straws trying to come up with a viable answer was not lost on Ethan. *Did she know? Wasn't she in bed? Or did she sneak out and see him and Olivia sitting on the porch swing? Did she see them holding hands? Or Olivia kissing him on the cheek?* He was pretty sure Emma didn't see him kissing Olivia goodnight after he walked her home.

"Yeah, we talked for a little bit."

"What about?"

"Oh, we mostly talked about you and how worried everyone was when we couldn't find you and Bella."

Emma rinsed another plate and handed it over without

looking at Ethan. "So you and Olivia were out looking for me and Bella?"

"Yep. We looked here, the garage, the orchard, the pier, and finally the lighthouse."

"It was just you and Olivia?"

Ethan closed the cupboard door. "Well, Audrey and her parents were also looking when Olivia told them she couldn't find Bella."

"But you and Olivia were both out there looking for me? Just you and her?"

"Yeah, it was just me and Olivia."

Ethan looked at Emma as she appeared to be completely engrossed in washing the last dirty dish. He thought she might have been trying hard to suppress a smile. Then she started humming a zippy tune he didn't recognize.

What was up with her? The more he tried to peer into that young brain of hers, the more curious he became. He thought about last night. He and Olivia looking everywhere for Emma. So unlike her to run off without telling him. Totally out of character. He never would have imagined it.

Wait a minute.

He took a step back. *Could it be? Did she plan the whole thing? Did she intentionally hide herself so Ethan and Olivia would be forced to search for her—just the two of them? Had he been the victim of some ornery nine-year-old's plot to bring him and the former love of his life back together?* He didn't put it past her.

"Emma, how would you like to go to the Tigers game tonight?"

Emma carefully removed her rubber gloves and hopped down from the step stool. "A game? A real live baseball game?"

"Yep. I think we ought to go see them in person, maybe bring them some good luck."

Emma clasped her hands together. "Oh, Mr. Ethan! I've never been to a real baseball game before. I would love to go!"

Ethan thought he might sweeten the pot a little. "I thought maybe we could invite Olivia to go with us."

Emma's eyes widened. "You want Olivia to go, too?"

"Yeah. The Tigers are playing the Dodgers. Olivia might not follow the game of baseball like you do, but since she used to live out in L.A., she might like to see the Dodgers."

She jumped up and gave him a hug. "I would love to go to a game with you and Olivia, Mr. Ethan. Thank you! Thank you!"

* * *

With only three people going, Ethan decided they'd make the three-hour trip to Detroit in his pickup. Emma squeezed into the middle, and Olivia sat next to her. With the warm summer air, all three of them went with shorts. Emma wore the Tigers shirt Ethan gave her for her birthday. Olivia wore a form-fitting Tigers tank top, and with her long tanned legs, it was hard for Ethan to concentrate on the road. Both his women wore a Tigers hat, and Ethan always thought there was nothing more attractive than a woman who could wear a ball cap.

As they sped down the interstate, Emma asked yet another one of her questions. "Did you two ever go to any games when you were going out?"

Ethan looked over at Olivia and Olivia looked back at him, each one trying to decide who should take this one.

"Let me see," Olivia said, tapping her finger to her chin. "I think we might have gone to a game once or twice."

Emma looked over at Ethan for his response.

Ethan leaned closer to speak to Emma. "Olivia wasn't much of a baseball fan."

Olivia feigned outrage. "That's not true! I used to come to your games at Michigan all the time. Don't you remember?"

Ethan had to admit she was correct. "I do remember. You came to most of my games, and I always appreciated it. I'd be standing out in centerfield and I could see you sitting in the stands." His mind drifted to remembering the times when he thought life couldn't get any better—a life with a bright future in baseball and Olivia by his side.

Olivia picked up where he left off. "Remember the time you hit that walk-off home run against Wisconsin? Everybody went crazy. Your teammates hoisted you on their shoulders and then all the fans charged onto the field to celebrate."

Emma's wide eyes looked at Ethan. "Did that really happen?"

Ethan closed his eyes just for a second, to relive the glory days. Hitting a home run in the bottom of the ninth inning to win the game and then to have his blonde-haired beauty of a girlfriend jump into his arms and give him a celebratory kiss was what dreams were made of. He would remember that moment of euphoria for as long as he lived. And to think, he was sitting in the truck with that very same blonde-haired beauty.

"Yeah," he said, looking over Emma to catch Olivia's eye. "That was one of those days that I'll never forget."

The trio walked into Comerica Park at the end of batting practice and took their seats down the third-base line. Emma took it all in—the massive ballpark, the green grass, the sights, the sounds, the smell of hot dogs and buttery popcorn. Ethan bought her some pink cotton candy, and they all had sticky fingers once it was gone. They stood and cheered when Emma's favorite player Jordan Foster hit a home run. Then they sang *Take Me Out to the Ball Game* during the seventh-inning stretch, and Ethan even caught a foul ball for Emma. Even better, the Tigers led by six runs going into the eighth.

"You ladies want anything else to eat or drink?" Ethan asked as the Dodgers came to bat.

Olivia shook her head and put her hand over her stomach. "No thanks. I had too much cotton candy."

"Emma?"

Before she could respond, her attention shot to the jumbotron TV. "Look!" she said pointing at the screen. "It's the Kiss Cam."

Ethan and Olivia looked up at the screen in time to see a man and a woman seated down the first-base line, their pictures appearing in a red heart on the screen, and the crowd rooting them to show some affection. Their kiss received applause, and the camera moved to another unsuspecting couple in the right-field bleachers. When the man looked at his seatmate and then hesitated to make his move, the crowd booed him lustily. Laughter ensued when his girlfriend gave him the what-are-you-waiting-for look. The guy quickly complied with a peck. The camera moved on, wanting to find one last kiss. It stopped on a threesome down the third-base line.

"Hey, look!" Emma said, pointing at the screen. "That's me! I'm on TV! I'm on TV!"

With Ethan, Emma, and Olivia all in the red heart, Ethan turned toward Olivia. They didn't have to say a word, their thoughts were the same. With Emma in the middle, Ethan planted a kiss on her left cheek and Olivia did the same on the right. The lasting image for the entire stadium was the cheesy grin of the cutest nine-year-old in the world and the couple lucky enough to be seated next to her.

* * *

With a firm hold on her prized souvenir that Ethan caught for her, Emma fell asleep somewhere between Detroit and Flint with Olivia's arm around her. With two hours to go, Ethan looked over at Olivia.

"You can go to sleep if you want."

Olivia turned her head. Her eyes showed she was tired, but she smiled. "I'm fine," she whispered. She glanced down at Emma. "I think she had a blast, Ethan. She'll remember this day forever."

Ethan reached out and squeezed Olivia's hand. He didn't say a word, and Olivia didn't need him to.

After the long three-hour drive, Ethan eased his truck to a stop outside his house. Emma was still fast asleep under Olivia's arm. Ethan whispered to Olivia. "Will you let me walk you home?"

Olivia reached out and touched his arm. "I'd like that."

Ethan carried Emma upstairs, got her dressed in her *I'm not tipsy, I'm from Ypsi* nightshirt, and tucked her and Wilfred into bed. She still had a hold of the baseball.

Once back outside, he found Olivia sitting on the porch railing. He just stood and admired her for a few seconds. Everything felt so right. Like all was right with the world. He walked closer and held out his hand. She took it and stood. Neither was ready to call it a night. He used his free hand to hold her close and he inhaled the sweet aroma of her strawberry-scented shampoo. He hadn't held her in his arms for years, but he remembered every beautiful and soft curve.

She locked eyes with him. "I had a wonderful time

tonight, Ethan."

Ethan could feel her body shivering. But the warm evening told him, Olivia wasn't cold. She was feeling the same things he was. He could feel her heart pounding through her tank top and against his chest. Or maybe it was his heart that was pounding.

"I can't remember the last time I had such an enjoyable evening, Olivia." Ethan didn't want it to end. He wanted to hold her in his arms and not let her go this time. "And it's all because of you."

Olivia leaned in closer. She focused her eyes on his handsome face. The tight jaw line, the deep dark eyes that penetrated her soul. Her smile raised her cheekbones. "I've missed being with you, Ethan."

Ethan dipped his head. "Not as much as I've missed you."

Olivia rose up on her toes. "We never actually got to show the world how much we missed each other on the Kiss Cam."

"I was thinking the same thing."

When their lips met, neither flinched, neither backed away. Each took the other in deeply to savor every second of the electric bond they shared. Olivia let out a slight moan as Ethan grabbed her even tighter to him. He backed her up, picked her up, and placed her on the porch railing. She didn't let go, and neither did he. He broke his contact with her lips and kissed her cheek, then moved down her neck.

"Ethan," she whispered into his ear.

With his heart pounding, Ethan paused to catch his breath. He rested his forehead against hers. The look in his eyes told her he wanted more, to show her how much he truly loved her. His grin said he knew he would have to wait, but that didn't mean he couldn't tell her his feelings.

"I want you, Olivia Daniels." He kissed her on her left cheek. "I want you in my life." He kissed her again on the right.

"I'm not going anywhere, Ethan Stone."

Their lips met again, and neither of them wanted to let go of the other.

CHAPTER 30

When Emma sat down at the kitchen table to enjoy her bowl of Frosted Flakes, the smile from the night before had yet to subside. Ethan had heard her humming a tune as she bounded down the stairs, and her first act upon entering the kitchen was to give him a tight hug.

"Did you have a good time last night?" Ethan asked between bites of cereal.

"Oh, yes. I had a great time. It was so much fun, and I can't believe you caught a foul ball for me."

Ethan smiled. "That's the first one I've ever caught. Right place, right time."

"Do you think Olivia had a good time?"

Ethan nodded. "I know she did because she told me. And she also told me how special of a girl you are."

Emma beamed.

"Olivia and I were talking and thought you and Bella might like to go see that new Disney movie."

Emma's eyes widened. Just hearing him mention Olivia's name and their plans together caused her to think going to see a movie was the greatest idea she had ever heard. "I would love to see the Disney movie. What time are we going to go? Are you going to sit by Olivia? It's okay if you want to. I can sit next to Bella. Maybe you and Olivia could share some popcorn. Could we get some ice cream afterwards? Or we could come back here and have some. I know Olivia likes chocolate ice cream." She clasped her hands together. "Oh, Mr. Ethan, I can't wait."

Emma ate her Frosted Flakes with hardly a word, her eyes gleaming and smiles abounding. Ethan knew full well the reasons. He could almost see the wheels spinning in her mind. After what happened on the Fourth of July, he couldn't help but grin at the thought of what she might have up her sleeve next.

* * *

With his pickup truck being his sole mode of transportation, and not wanting to squeeze four people into the front seat of the cab, Ethan suggested Olivia drive her Mustang. And with the warm Michigan summer, Olivia had the top down so all could enjoy the breezes.

Olivia didn't even have to honk before Emma flew out the door. The time had finally arrived, and Emma was ready to go. She hopped in the back with Bella, and Ethan glided down into the front passenger seat. The growl of the Mustang's V8 engine announced their departure.

With her blonde tresses blowing in the wind, Olivia glanced to her right. "It's been a while since we've gone to the movies, hasn't it?"

Ethan turned his head and found Olivia smiling at him. "Yeah. It has been a while."

"Do you remember the first movie we saw together?"

Ethan laughed. "Don't try to fool me with your trick questions. I know exactly which movie we saw."

"What was it?"

"It was *Snow White and Seven Dwarfs*."

"Oh my . . . ," Olivia said, her jaw dropping before breaking into a laugh. "I can't believe you remember that. We were like seven years old!"

"Yep. I think my parents were out of town and your parents wanted to get everyone, including me, out of their house for the afternoon, so they dropped us all off at the mall and told us to go see a movie. *Snow White* was the only movie we could get into."

Olivia smiled at the memory. "That was the first of many movies over the years."

Ethan was lost in thought for a moment as he watched the countryside go by. "Yeah, a lot of movies."

"You always liked the action ones."

Breaking out of his trance, he looked over at Olivia. "And you had a thing for the tearjerkers."

Emma and Bella giggled to each other in the back seat.

The four of them sat in the middle of the theater—Olivia on one end and Ethan on the other with the two girls in between them. Bella and Emma shared a bucket of popcorn. Halfway through the movie, Olivia rested her arm on the back of Bella's seat. Ethan did the same with Emma, and his hand met Olivia's in the middle. In the darkness, he slowly ran his finger against Olivia's forearm, the touch feeling so right. The whole day felt right. And with the time they spent together yesterday at the ball game, everything felt right. This was what he had always wanted. This was as close as he had ever come to having a family. A wife and two daughters. He'd be okay with that. He glanced over at Olivia. It didn't take her long to feel his eyes on her. When she glanced over, Ethan winked at her. In the darkness of the theater, he could still see the love of his life blush.

* * *

Olivia dabbed at her chocolate ice cream. The cup was half empty, but she couldn't eat much more. She placed her hand on her stomach, trying to will away the pain going on inside of her. But it had nothing to do with ice cream.

She couldn't remember the last time she felt so conflicted. No wait, yes she could. It was two years ago. Ethan had proposed to her, saying he wanted to spend the rest of his life with her. She, however, had another offer. Gerard Cologne had promised to make her a star if only she accompanied him to Hollywood. She was at a fork in the road of life. Should she take the road where she would spend the rest of her life in Michigan with the man who loved her with all his heart? Or should she latch on to a man who had his own reasons for tempting her with the intoxicating elixir of fame and fortune? She chose the latter, and yet here she was sitting on a park bench in Huron Cove eating ice cream with Ethan Stone.

Is this what she wanted?

"Emma's going to be disappointed when Bella goes home at the end of summer vacation," Ethan said to Olivia.

Olivia dropped the spoon in her cup. Emma and Bella had already eaten and were running off excess energy on the jungle gym.

When Olivia didn't answer, Ethan snapped his fingers in front of her face. "You still with me?"

Olivia snapped out of it. "What?"

"You still with me? I said I bet Emma's going to be disappointed when Bella goes back to Grand Rapids."

The statement finally got through to Olivia's brain. "Oh, yeah. I'm sure they'll both miss each other."

"You kind of spaced out there for a moment. Something on your mind."

Olivia watched as Bella and Emma raced over to the swing set. "I'm sorry. I was just thinking about the movie."

"You didn't like it?"

Olivia leaned forward and rested her elbows on her knees. "Oh, I liked it." She sounded far from enthused.

Ethan leaned forward, too. "What's wrong?"

Olivia shook her head. This had been the first movie she had watched since leaving Hollywood, and the pain of what might have been twisted her stomach into knots. *Would it be like this whenever she went to a movie?* "You know Arianna Cole?"

"The actress in the movie?"

"Yeah." Olivia sat back on the bench and looked over at Ethan. "I know her." She refrained from telling Ethan that she had Cole's number on speed dial. They even had the same agent. She looked away so he wouldn't see the tear rolling down her cheek.

Ethan scooted closer and put his arm around her. "It's tough for you, isn't it? To see someone on the big screen like that when it has been your dream to do the same?"

She did her best to choke back her tears. "Yeah. It's real tough."

Ethan rubbed her back. "But you were up there on the big screen and on TV. You're a star and always will be."

She shook her head, not wanting to agree with him.

"You are, Olivia. You came from little ol' Huron Cove, Michigan, and made it big. Nobody can take that away from you. Maybe your time in Hollywood is over, but you're still the brightest star here. And you're going to put Huron Cove on the map with your family's B and B."

She took a deep breath and gave Ethan a nod to let him know she appreciated his sentiments.

He leaned in closer and whispered into her ear. "And you got me, too." He stopped to take a deep breath. "You mean the world to me, Olivia. I've never stopped loving you. I was angry, yes, but I never stopped loving you. I want you to be happy. And I want you to be happy here."

Olivia blinked away tears. *Was she fully committed to this life now? Was she ready to give up her dreams of becoming a star in Hollywood and to live a life as a B&B operator in Huron Cove, Michigan?*

She didn't know how to answer.

CHAPTER 31

"You're really quiet today," Emma said to Ethan.

Ethan thought he heard Emma say something, but it went in one ear and out the other. Maybe it was the wind rushing in through the open window of the pickup or maybe he was distracted by the small amount of traffic heading toward Huron Cove.

Or maybe it had everything to do with Olivia Daniels.

"I'm sorry, what?"

"I said you're really quiet today. You didn't comment about the Tigers winning their third in a row last night. And you didn't say anything when I told you Michigan is the Wolverine State even though there aren't any wolverines around anymore."

Ethan tapped the steering wheel with the fingers on his left hand. "Yeah, tigers and wolverines. That's interesting."

Emma leaned forward and to her left to try and look Ethan in the eye. "What's wrong?"

He didn't make eye contact with her. He just shook his head and said, "Nothing."

She reached out and patted his arm. "It's obvious something is bothering you."

He looked over and saw those big brown eyes again. He needed to stop doing that. He sighed. "It's obvious, huh?"

"Yeah. You're very tense, like something is gnawing at your gut."

Ethan did a double take. "Gnawing at my gut?"

"That's what Aunt Millie used to say. It means that something's eating away at you on the inside, like you can't figure something out or you don't know what the answer is to your problem."

"I don't know what the answer is, Emma. And *it is* bothering me."

"It's about Olivia, isn't it?

"You can read me like a book, can't you?"

Emma shrugged. "There isn't much else. It either has to do with me, work, or Olivia." She thought some more before adding, "Or the Tigers. But they're so bad this year that it's pretty much narrowed down to me, work, or Olivia."

Ethan blew out a breath. He flicked on his turn signal and took a right at the stop sign. "Yeah, it has to do with Olivia."

Emma smiled. "Maybe I can help."

Ethan couldn't help but wonder if he really did know the answer. He had let Olivia Daniels back into his life, and, truth be told, he loved it. He loved hanging out with her, working with her, and going to movies with her. He loved her and always would. But there was something in the deep recesses of his mind that told him not to go any farther. He had been fighting the urge to give in to what in his heart he knew was right.

"I don't know what's going on with Olivia right now, Emma."

"Because you still like her, don't you?"

Ethan shook his head. "Like" didn't describe what he felt in terms of Olivia. He had given his heart over to her once before, and now he felt like he was racing out of control down a hill. He didn't know whether he could stop the freefall or even if he wanted to stop. "I'll always have feelings for Olivia. And I really don't know whether she has the same type of feelings for me that I have for her. That's one of the things that I can't figure out."

"And you're afraid to take the chance again. Afraid that she's going to break your heart."

This time it was Ethan who reached over and patted Emma on the hand. "You are wise beyond your years, Emma Lynn."

"Why don't you ask her to marry you?"

Being struck by lightning would not have caused a greater jolt to his body than Emma's question. To keep from running off the road, Ethan grabbed the steering wheel with both hands and let his foot off the gas. Thinking better of it, he pulled the truck to a stop in the parking lot of a gas station.

It was like she could read his mind. He wanted to ask Olivia to marry him. He thought about it all night. He knew Olivia was struggling to decide what she wanted out of her life. But there was one thing for sure he wanted out of his. He wanted Olivia to be his wife. And together, they could raise Emma as a family. Maybe it would work this time. He would do anything to make it work. But would it be enough for Olivia? He rubbed his hand across his face and then the back of his neck but said nothing.

"Mr. Ethan, Olivia is kind of like your Anne."

His confusion with her statement brought his mind back to focus. "My what?"

"Your Anne." She held up the latest book she was reading—*Anne of Avonlea*. "She's like Anne Shirley, and you're her Gilbert Blythe. You were meant for each other. You two are meant to live a long and loving life together."

He smiled and closed his eyes at the memories of what could have been. They were happy memories, full of smiles and love, except for when Olivia left him. He opened his eyes and said, "I thought that exact same thing once before, Emma. And look how that turned out."

"But this is different. You two are older now. Olivia went out to Hollywood and came back home. You're here, and she needs you."

He pulled the shoulder belt away from his chest to give him some breathing room. "She needs me, huh?"

Emma nodded. "I think you need her, too. Now's your chance."

He tried to counterpoint, to talk himself out of what he wanted to do. "I already took that chance."

"But this one might be your last. You may never have this chance again."

Ethan gave Emma a good long look. What a whirlwind couple weeks it had been—Emma making her appearance into his life and Olivia coming back to Huron Cove. Now he sat in his pickup truck with the most wonderful nine-year-old girl he could ever imagine. She needed a woman in her life, someone she could call her mother. He also needed a woman in his life, someone he could call his wife.

The answer to his dilemma eluded him. He only had one place else to turn. He reached out for Emma's hand. "Maybe we should pray about it."

It didn't take long after the conclusion of the prayer for Ethan to make his decision. He just needed a little push, and talking with Emma, and with God, told him it was the right thing to do. Now Ethan and Emma were back on the road with a purpose.

"Aren't we going into town?" Emma asked as Ethan turned onto the interstate heading south.

Ethan gave her a wide smile. "The best jewelry store around is in Saginaw."

Emma gasped, her hands covering her mouth. "You're going to ask Olivia to marry you!" Receiving the confirmation from Ethan unleashed a torrent of feelings from Emma. "I'm so excited! I can't wait. Can I help you pick out the ring?"

"Of course, that's why I'm bringing you with me."

"And then you're going to get married and have a wedding ceremony. Maybe at the lake with a reception in the barn that you fixed up. And there'll be flowers and candles and a wedding cake. I'm so excited I could burst."

Ethan laughed. "I'm glad you're excited because I'm excited, too."

"When are you going to ask her?"

Ethan tapped his fingers on the steering wheel. He didn't feel the need to wait. "Why don't I ask her tonight when we get back?"

Emma could barely contain herself, and the only thing that kept her from sticking her head out the window to shout for joy was her securely fastened seat belt. "Does that mean we can sit by her at church tomorrow?"

"Emma, if she says yes, we can sit by her every Sunday."

CHAPTER 32

"You sure have been quiet today, Olivia," Beth said as her sister walked into the kitchen. "I thought you might have gone into town with Ethan and Emma."

Olivia put her cell phone on the counter and took a seat on the stool. She had spent the morning walking up and down the shores of Lake Huron. She barely slept the night before, and the mental and physical exhaustion was weighing her down. Although she wasn't sure whether she wanted to talk at all right now, she knew her sister would pester her until she squeezed the information out of her. Still, she looked down at her manicured nails, hoping to avoid the subject.

"Did you and Ethan have a good time at the movies last night?"

Olivia nodded. "Yeah."

Beth put a glass of iced tea in front of Olivia. "So what's wrong?"

Olivia wrapped her hands around the cold glass and shrugged. "Nothing's wrong."

Beth sat down next to her. "Liar."

"No, really. Nothing's wrong." Olivia cast her gaze to the floor. She couldn't even convince herself that what she said was true.

"Olivia, I might be the baby of the family, but that doesn't mean I'm so naïve that I can't see the signs. Something's bothering you. Olivia Daniels doesn't go through the doldrums like normal people. She's too bright a star to have black clouds of despair hovering over her." Beth reached out and laid her hand on Olivia's forearm. "And seeing that I'm the only one here, you're going to have to tell me what's causing you to be so upset."

Olivia sighed. Maybe talking about it would help. "I was sitting in the theater yesterday with Ethan and the girls." She looked out the window toward Ethan's house. "And then there was Arianna Cole on the screen."

"Your friend?"

Olivia nodded. "It was so hard to see her. I almost felt sick to my stomach. Don't get me wrong, I'm happy for her but . . ."

"You wanted it to be you."

Olivia rested her head in her hand. She couldn't disagree. "I wanted to be the one on that screen. The one that people say is the greatest actress in the world. I wanted to be the one on the cover of magazines and the subject of all the entertainment shows. I wanted to walk down the red carpet and be blinded by a million flashbulbs as people shouted my name."

She couldn't bring herself to say what she was really thinking. *Instead, I'm an out-of-work actress living in my parents' house in Huron Cove, Michigan.*

"But you're loved here, Olivia. Everyone in town loves you. We all love you. And we love having you around. You're doing a wonderful job with the B and B. Mom and Dad both say this place is going to survive because of you."

Olivia managed a thankful smile. "You sound like Ethan."

Beth grabbed hold of Olivia's hand. "Ethan's a wonderful guy, and it's clear as day that he still has feelings for you. Have you thought about getting back together with him? I mean long-term."

Olivia nodded. The images in her head went back and forth between her and Ethan and Ethan and Emma. "I can't stop thinking about it. I know he loves me . . . but. . . I don't know."

"Have you prayed about it?"

Olivia couldn't stop the tears from rolling down her cheeks. She nodded, her eyes reddening. "I've prayed, but I still don't know what to do."

Beth stood up and wrapped her arms around her sister. "God will provide the answer when it's time, Olivia. You just have to be patient and put your trust in Him."

Olivia choked back tears. She unwrapped an arm from Beth's embrace and hugged her sister tight. "How'd you get so smart?"

Beth patted Olivia on the back. "I have two older sisters who were the greatest teachers in the world."

"Thank you for listening," Olivia said, wiping the tears from her cheeks. "And thanks for the advice."

"You gonna be okay?"

Olivia took a deep cleansing breath. "Yeah. I just need to pray some more and be patient. Just like you said." Now it was time for her to be the big sister. "You probably better get ready for your date tonight."

"Are you sure? I can call Luke and tell him I can't make it tonight."

Olivia would have none of that. She was a big girl. "Go get ready. I'll be fine. A little more alone time will help me clear my head. And Ethan said he and Emma wouldn't be back until sometime early this evening."

The two sisters hugged again, and Beth went upstairs to get ready. Olivia sat back down at the counter and took a sip of iced tea. She could see Ethan's house from her perch, and she knew he and Emma had yet to return based on the empty driveway. *What did she want?* She thought she wanted to give up acting and run the B&B. *But is that really what she wanted?* She squeezed her eyes shut and balled her fists.

Olivia flinched and then froze when her phone sang the tune for *Hooray for Hollywood*. She didn't pick it up. She didn't even look who the caller was. She knew. She hadn't heard that tune for almost a year, and she couldn't believe it was still even on her phone. She felt her pulse picking up, and her hands started to shake. *Should she answer it?* Her chest rose and fell like she was going to hyperventilate. *Is this how alcoholics feel when someone puts a drink in front of them?* The temptation was paralyzing. *What did she want?* Was Ethan the answer to all of her prayers? Or was it someone else? Someone she had fallen for once before. *Is that who she wanted?* She opened her eyes and looked at the screen. She swallowed hard. With the song still filling her ears, she reached out, grabbed the phone, and took a deep breath. Then she tapped the button.

"Hello?" She closed her eyes at hearing the man on the other end. "It's good to hear your voice too, Gerard."

CHAPTER 33

Ethan couldn't help but smile at Emma's joyful enthusiasm. She was so excited about the prospect of Ethan popping the question that she could barely sit still in the truck on the way back from Saginaw. They had picked out a stunning three-stone diamond ring that glistened in the light. Emma took one look at the jewel sparkling in the display case and pronounced it to be the perfect ring for Olivia Daniels. As the ring's radiance was befitting the intended recipient, Ethan wholeheartedly agreed.

"Are you going to tell her you love her?" Emma asked. Her legs kicked the air in front of her, unable to keep still for even a second.

Ethan looked over at his passenger. "I have a pretty good feeling that sentiment might come up."

Emma smiled bigger, if that was possible. "That's good. Women like it when you tell them you love them. And how beautiful they are. And how happy you make them. Just don't jump up and down on the couch when you're doing it."

Ethan had to do a double-take on that one. "Don't what?"

"There was a guy on Oprah. He really liked this girl he was dating, and he started jumping up and down on Oprah's couch saying how much he loved the woman."

"Really?"

"Yeah. People thought it was weird."

"Okay. Well then, I'll stay off the couch when I ask her. I thought I might see if Olivia will take a walk along the lake with me."

"That's perfect. And so romantic. I'll stay at the house. That way you two can have some time alone. But do come back quickly when she says yes, because I don't think I can keep it all bottled up inside me for very long."

Ethan took note that Emma had no hesitation that Olivia would say yes. He reached over and patted her on the arm. "You'll be the first person we tell the good news. Then you can announce it to everyone."

The only bad thing about the chatterbox known as Emma Lynn Grayson was she didn't give Ethan much time to gather his thoughts. He was just about to ask the love of his life to marry him. Again. There was so much different the second time around. The new ring for one thing. But, more importantly, he was sure now more than ever that asking Olivia Daniels to marry him was the right thing to do. He wanted her in his life. He needed her in his life. And he wanted to spend the rest of his life showing her how much he loved her.

"Are you nervous?" Emma asked, breaking his thoughts.

Given the sweaty shirt he was wearing and the constant drumming of his fingers on the steering wheel, he couldn't lie about it. "A little bit." He looked at the speedometer and pressed harder on the gas pedal. Only thirty more miles separated him from the love of his life.

"I think that's normal."

Ethan smiled. "I think I heard that some guys get a little nervous on the big day."

"Thanks for letting me come along to help you pick out the ring."

For once Emma took a breath and waited for his response. Ethan looked over at her—the big brown eyes, the endearing smile, the heart of gold. *Why had God brought her into his life?* He wasn't for sure the reason, but he would be forever thankful for this blessing. "Well, thank you for being who you are, Emma. I don't know whether I'd be on the verge of asking Olivia to marry me if it weren't for you bringing us back together."

Emma smiled some more and then leaned over. "Can't this thing go any faster?"

Ethan just about sent Emma into a tizzy when he announced he was going to have to stop for gas. Not much he could do, unless they wanted to be stranded on the side of the road. He pulled the truck off the interstate and stopped at the first gas station he could find. Emma didn't even unbuckle her seatbelt, and she declined Ethan's offer for a soda or anything to eat.

"Now's no time to eat!" she yelled to Ethan as he stood outside the truck and pumped the fuel. "There's a proposal awaitin'!"

Back in the truck with a full load of fuel and now cruising down the interstate toward Huron Cove, Ethan could feel his grip loosening on the leather steering wheel. The nerves were kicking in, and wiping his palms on his jeans didn't seem to help. "Say something, Emma. I need a distraction for the last twenty miles."

Emma obliged. "It's too bad you couldn't have asked her on the Fourth of July. Then there could have been fireworks in celebration."

Ethan laughed. "Well, I was kind of busy looking for you that night. And, in reality, I wasn't ready yet. But being with Olivia looking for you and then talking with her afterwards made me realize that I couldn't let her go for a second time. And hanging out with you and her at the ball game and the movie told me she's the only one for me. So, the Fourth won't be an anniversary, but maybe the fireworks will remind us of the night Olivia and I got back together."

Ethan craned his neck to look out the truck's front windshield. He had hoped to make it back to Huron Cove before the sun set, but Mother Nature had different plans. A gray cloud layer was blowing in from the northwest, and the forecast called for a drop in temperature and showers to start later on that night and last through the next day.

"Finally," Emma said as Ethan parked the truck outside the house. She unbuckled her seatbelt. "Can we go over right now?"

Ethan walked around the back of the truck. He looked over at the Daniels' house and saw the lights were on. He glanced skyward to judge the weather. "I think we have some time before the rain hits, and I need take a quick shower." He could see the pain of forcing her to wait another minute. "Why don't you go to the garden and pick some flowers to give to Olivia."

Ten minutes later, Ethan walked out onto the porch and looked at the lighthouse to the north. The rays from its spinning light reflected off the gray and darkening cloud layer. He went with the blue button-down with the long sleeves. If he waited any longer, he was going to have to bring a jacket.

"Emma?"

He heard the scampering of feet from beside the house.

"I'm right here!" She appeared with a bouquet of flowers that looked like it had once consumed half the garden. "Are you ready?"

Ethan stepped down from the porch. "I'm ready. You get enough flowers?"

"I think so. Do you think Olivia will like them?"

"No," he said. He waited for the shock to appear in her eyes and then said, "She'll *love* them, Emma."

She smiled. "Do you have the ring?"

Ethan patted the pocket of his slacks. "Right here."

"Well, let's go then!"

They headed toward the Daniels' house, and Emma had to restrain herself from skipping too far ahead of Ethan.

She turned and walked backwards as she looked at him. "Do you think I can be a flower girl at the wedding?"

When he caught up to her, Ethan wrapped his arm around her shoulder. "I think that can be arranged. You'll be the most beautiful flower girl ever."

Emma didn't respond with any more questions, giving Ethan a moment to collect his thoughts. They passed over into the Daniels' yard. Olivia's Mustang wasn't in the driveway, and Ethan figured she wanted to get it in the garage before the rain came.

They stopped once they reached the front porch steps. Ethan turned to his young companion. "Wish me luck."

Emma was nearly speechless at the moment, but she managed a whisper. "Good luck." She nodded to the side of the porch. "I'll stand over there until you head to the lake."

Ethan strode confidently up the stairs and crossed the front porch. He knocked twice and waited for the love of his life to appear.

Instead, Beth showed up at the door and opened it.

"Is Olivia here?"

Beth looked hard at him but shook her head. In an instant, Ethan felt a twinge in his stomach.

"I hate to be the one to tell you this, Ethan." A tear rolled down her cheek. "Gerard called. Olivia left for California a couple of hours ago."

Ethan could feel his jaws tighten. His nostrils flared as he tried to make sense of what she just said. He looked down at the floorboards of the porch and tried to stop the explosion of feelings overloading his brain. The hollow feeling in his heart had been felt once before, and soon the pain would start all over again. He closed his eyes and shook his head.

"I'm so sorry, Ethan," Beth whispered.

Ethan nodded. He could take the punch to the gut. He had done so before. But it was different this time around. There was someone else who desperately wanted Olivia's love. The sniffles coming from the end of the porch broke his heart. He didn't even have to break the news to Emma. She already knew. When the door closed softly behind him, he walked down the steps and found Emma crying into her bouquet of flowers.

"Let's go home, Emma."

Once they left the Daniels' yard, Emma, try as she might, couldn't keep her emotions inside her any longer. She tossed the bouquet of flowers to the ground. She covered her face with her hands and started sobbing.

Ethan gritted his teeth—upset at himself for allowing Emma to get her hopes up. He should have known better. He should have never let it happen. *What kind of a father was he?* He bent down, picked her up, and wrapped her in his arms. She held on to him like she would never let go. "I'm sorry, Emma," he whispered into her ear. He could feel her tears running down the side of his neck. "I'm so sorry."

CHAPTER 34

When he woke up the next morning, Ethan had no idea how many hours he had slept. It wasn't many—two at the most. He finally got Emma calmed down, and she ended up crying herself to sleep. He spent most of the night staring at the ceiling, furious at himself that he would open the door to his heart only to have Olivia crush it yet again. *What was he thinking?* But causing Emma pain was the worst part of it. That was hard for him to take.

So many questions were left unanswered. What was he going to do now? What happens when Olivia comes back to visit? Should he keep Emma away from the Daniels' house? He had no idea if Olivia had gotten a part or whether she just jetted off to shack up with her French beau. He didn't want to know. There were no messages or texts on his phone, and he decided to turn it off and put it in the drawer for the day. If Olivia wanted to call and apologize, or at least give him a reason for dumping him and breaking Emma's heart in the process, she could do it when he was good and ready. Until then, Olivia Daniels was once again officially off limits. This time—forever.

He looked at his watch. Seven o'clock. He rubbed his tired face, and when he looked toward the end of the bed, he realized he had slept in his clothes. At least his shoes were off. With a low groan, he urged his stiff legs off the bed. He then sat up and rested his arms on his knees. Seven o'clock in the morning. The morning after. The Sunday morning after. He sighed and thought of Emma. Olivia might have let her down by not even saying goodbye before she left, but Ethan Stone wasn't going to break that little girl's heart. He was responsible for her now, and he was going to do everything he could to help her through the pain she was experiencing.

After a long, hot shower, he put on a dark pair of slacks and a white dress shirt. He walked down the hall and eased into Emma's bedroom. His stomach dropped when he saw she was still in bed, facing away from the door, the sheets and blankets a disorganized pile on the floor. He sat down on the edge of the bed and took a breath.

"Emma," he said, rubbing her arm to wake her. "Wake up. It's time to go to church."

Emma had Wilfred E. Goodbear clutched tight against her chest. She didn't respond. Ethan saw her baseball had rolled to a stop in the corner. He also noticed Olivia's framed picture was laying face down on her dresser. Ethan gave her another little shake. When Emma rolled over, Ethan could tell she had been crying. It broke his heart.

"Time to go to church."

"I don't want to go to church!" She rolled away from him and clutched Wilfred tighter.

He wondered what Oprah would say. It didn't take him long to realize the moment was too important for words of Oprah's wisdom. He needed the Lord's help. Now more than ever. In a silent prayer, he asked God to provide him with the right thing to say to help heal his little girl's pain.

He rubbed her arm again. "Emma," he said softly. "The Lord's waiting for us."

He could tell by the flinch that she felt the words in her heart. They were the same words she had used on him that first Sunday they were together. She rolled over and looked at him with her red eyes. Tear stains lined her cheeks.

He opened his arms wide. "Come here."

She scrambled up and wrapped her arms around him without saying a word. He could feel the tightness in her squeeze.

"I'm sorry again, Emma. Sometimes life doesn't always work out the way we want it to. There are good days and bad days. Some days can feel like you're on top of the highest mountain, and the next it feels like you're down in the deepest valley." He rubbed her back some more and then turned his head to look at her. "But you know one thing that's for certain?"

"What?" she whispered.

"What's that Bible verse high above the altar at church?" He waited for her to respond. He could tell she knew it, but she didn't want to say it. "Do you remember it?"

She shook her head in the negative.

"Nah, come on now. I know you remember the verse I'm talking about. What does it say?"

She sniffled once before saying, "Lo, I am with you always."

Ethan smiled, the tears welling up in his own eyes. "That's right. Lo, I am with you always. No matter what happens in life, no matter what mountain we're on or what valley we're in, God is with us every step of the way. He'll get us through this. And as long as we have the Lord by our side, and we have each other to lean on, we'll get through it. Okay?"

She reached up to wipe a tear sliding down her cheek. "Okay," she whispered.

Ethan patted her on the back. "All right. Well, why don't you get ready for church, and I'll head downstairs to fix us a couple of bowls of Frosted Flakes and warm up some of Arlene's chocolate muffins. How's that sound?"

For the first time of the morning, Emma managed a weak smile.

They said little at the table, and the ride to church was quiet. Too quiet for Ethan. He knew someday he would have to ask her if she wanted to talk about it and what she was feeling in her heart. But for now, he thought they would just enjoy the warm Michigan breezes.

Ethan and Emma took their spot in the back row, and both of them noticed the Daniels family was absent. Mr. and Mrs. Daniels had gone to Grand Rapids with Audrey and Bella, and Beth had gone back to Ann Arbor. Olivia was just gone.

After a reading from Psalm twenty-three, Pastor Carlton announced the next scripture passage was from Romans, chapter eight.

Knowing the verses likely to be read, Ethan feigned ignorance and handed the Bible to Emma. "Can you find that for me?" he asked her.

Emma flipped through the Bible and found it just as Pastor Carlton began reading. She used her index finger to follow along.

"'For I am convinced that neither death nor life, neither angels nor demons, neither the present or the future, nor any powers, neither height nor depth, nor anything else in all creation, will be able to separate us from the love of God that is in Christ Jesus our Lord.'"

When she looked up at Ethan, he gave her a wink and a smile. When the sermon started, Ethan put his arm around her and held her close as they listened to Pastor Carlton.

"Far too many of us believe God is some sort of magic genie—one whom we need only rub the lamp of life a couple of times and wait for Him to rise up and grant our every wish. But it doesn't work that way. God's job is not to serve us. Instead, we are to serve Him in all that we do, giving thanks and praise for the blessings He has bestowed on us. Sure, it may be difficult to thank Him when times are bad—when the bills are piling up, when the pain of sickness and the sting of death reach our families, when spouses fight amongst themselves. But it is during those times that we must rely on God even more—thankful that we have Him to hear us as we bring our concerns to Him in prayer."

Ethan left church with his heart mended, the words of Pastor Carlton keeping his focus where it needed to be. He could tell by the energy in her steps that Emma felt it, too. They would move on and, with a lot of prayer, they would get past this.

"So, what do you want to do today, Emma?"

Emma looked out the window of the truck. Bella was away. Olivia was gone. It was just her and Ethan. She looked over at him and shrugged. "I don't care. What do you want to do?"

"Why don't we have some lunch and then we can play some catch. Maybe you can try out your new bat."

"Okay."

"I can hit you some grounders too, so you can work on your fielding."

"Do you think I can play on a team someday?"

Ethan came to a stop at the red light. He had to constantly remind himself that he needed to start thinking long-term when it came to Emma. It was the middle of July. In a month, Emma would have to start school. He was going to have to sign her up and buy her supplies. And she was going to need check-ups and a trip to the dentist. Before long, she'd have to learn how to drive and then there will be boys interested in her. Then there will be college and more boys and then a wedding!

"The light's green," Emma said.

Ethan shook. "Oh." He glanced in his rearview mirror but saw no one.

"So, can I?"

Ethan looked over at her and smiled. "Sure. I think there are some teams that play a few games in the early fall. I'll check with your school to see if they have a team." Ethan could barely believe it. His daughter was going to be a ballplayer just like him.

After a lunch of triangle PB&Js and a few innings of the Tigers game on TV, Ethan and Emma headed out to the south side of the house. Underneath the bright mid-afternoon sunshine, Ethan marked out the distance for the bases and pitching rubber so they could have their own field to practice on. They warmed up by playing catch.

"We'll have to work on your softball pitching one of these days," Ethan said as he caught a fastball from Emma. "And maybe we'll work on switch hitting."

Emma caught the return throw. "You mean you want me to bat left-handed, too?"

"Yeah. It'll be good to learn. Left-handed batters are quicker to first base. God blessed you with good speed, so you ought to use it to your advantage."

Ethan could see the sparkle in her eye, and it gave him a warm feeling in his heart. They would get through this. Baby steps. One day at a time. They would get through their heartache—together as a father and daughter.

Emma popped her glove twice with her fist. "Can I go get that foul ball you caught for me so we can throw it around?"

"Sure."

While Emma ran inside to retrieve the ball, Ethan walked to the side of the house, turned on the hose, and took a drink. He was surprised to hear a car door slam, having not even heard it pull up on the other side of the house. He thought it was probably Curt showing up unannounced. Maybe Ethan could enlist him to shag fly balls if Emma wanted to practice her hitting. He turned off the hose and started toward the front. Upon seeing the blonde-haired woman rounding the corner, he froze in his tracks. The ball he was holding fell to the grass with a thump. The blood rushed to his toes, and he stumbled before regaining his balance.

"Hi, Ethan."

The water from the hose had vanished in his now-dry mouth. He could feel his hands starting to shake, and his out-of-control heart raced in his chest. *This can't be happening. Not now. Not today. Not ever!* The woman stopped when she was ten feet from him.

"Miss White, what are you doing here?"

CHAPTER 35

"You're not answering your phone again, Ethan," Miss White said, frowning and shaking her head. "I've been trying to contact you all day."

Ethan could feel his mind spinning out of control. "What are you doing here?"

"I'm here to tell you the good news." Miss White smiled and took a step closer. "It took me awhile but just last night I finally found a good family for Emma, and I didn't want to wait another day to tell you."

Hitting him in the chest with a sledgehammer would not have struck him as deeply as Miss White's words. He staggered, his wobbly legs feeling like rubber. "What?"

"A family for Emma. That's what you wanted, isn't it, Ethan? It's a husband and wife with two kids of their own—both girls. Ron and Lacy Sherman. Great people. They live in Saginaw, and they're willing to take Emma off your hands."

Ethan felt like the blood had been drained from his body, the news stunning him to his core. *They're going to take his Emma away from him.* "I don't know what to say."

"I can get the paperwork started." She motioned toward the front of the house with her thumb. "Ron and Lacy followed me here if you want to meet them."

The peaceful silence of the Michigan afternoon was shattered by the painful screams of a nine-year-old girl. Emma had walked down with her baseball, saw a couple sitting in one of two cars sitting in the driveway, and then saw Ethan talking to Miss White.

"No! No!" Emma yelled as she burst out of the house. "Don't let her take me!" She barreled into Ethan and wrapped herself around his leg. "Please! Mr. Stone! . . . Mr. Ethan! . . . Daddy! Please, don't let her take me away!"

Ethan didn't try to pry Emma off of him. He reached down with his arm and held her even closer if that was possible. He looked at Miss White. "She's not going anywhere. She's staying with me."

A frazzled Miss White gulped. She didn't like the turn of events. It wasn't good for the child. With Emma crying and babbling something incoherent, she thought she could try to talk with Ethan. "You said you wanted me to find a good family for her."

"I changed my mind."

"Ethan, you said it yourself. Emma needs a mother and a father to love her." She tried to bring Ethan back to reality. "You said you could barely take care of yourself."

"Yeah, but. That was before . . ." He looked down at Emma.

"You don't want to be a single father, do you?"

The question reverberated through the trees, and the answer came from afar.

"He's not going to be a single father!"

In the suddenly surreal world that was Huron Cove, Michigan, the female voice came out of nowhere. It wasn't Emma, and it wasn't Miss White. It came from behind him, and when Ethan turned, his heart nearly stopped.

"At least not if I have anything to do about it."

The woman's voice and Ethan's turn toward the north caused Emma to open her eyes. "Miss Olivia!" She unwrapped herself from Ethan's leg, took off for Olivia, and jumped into her arms.

With Emma held tight, Olivia walked toward Ethan and Miss White. She locked eyes with the love of her life. "I'm back, Ethan. I'm back for good. I want to start a family, and I want it to be with you."

Miss White took a step back, unsure of what was going on. With the dumbfounded look on his face, Ethan wasn't sure what was going on either.

"Gerard called me, Ethan. He wanted me back. He said he had a part all lined up for me in a commercial." She looked down to find the right words. "I flew out to California yesterday, thinking I would do the commercial and see what Gerard had to say. But I never met with him. I sat in my apartment all night last night thinking about life. I don't think I slept at all. Then early this morning I realized you and Emma were probably on your way to church. But I wasn't. There aren't a whole lot of churches near my apartment, so the only thing I could think to do was kneel beside my bed and pray to God. All I could think about was you and Emma. I missed being home. And I missed both of you. This is where my heart is. This is where I want to be." She rubbed Emma's back. "I'm sorry if I hurt you Emma. And you too, Ethan. My mind was going a million miles an hour. But I'm back. I packed up the rest of my clothes in my apartment and took the first flight home. I tried to call you. I also told my agent that my career is now full-time in Huron Cove. My life is here, and I want to share my life with you."

Ethan took a step closer to Olivia. Words escaped him. He reached out his arm and pulled Olivia and Emma close to him. Then he wrapped both of his arms around them. The wash of serenity hit him, and he could sense they felt it too. This was the way it was meant to be.

"I love you, Ethan."

Ethan finally found the words deep in his heart. "I love

you too, Olivia."

He peeled Emma off Olivia, bent down, and whispered in the girl's ear. "You know where it is?" She nodded, smiled her beautiful smile, and took off again for the house.

Ethan grabbed hold of Olivia's hand and looked into her eyes. He brushed a strand of blonde hair out of her face. "I love you, Olivia. More than you'll ever know."

"I'm sorry for breaking your heart, Ethan. I was blinded by the bright lights of Hollywood. I fell for superficial love, for the hopes of adulation and praise. But I actually think I found my true self out there. What really matters is right here—faith, family . . . and you. Nothing can match the love of your best friend and man of your dreams. I want to be a family. I want to be your wife. I want you to be my husband."

"I'm not a party of one any longer."

"I want you and Emma to be in my life forever."

Ethan's grin spread across his face. "I'm one step ahead of you."

Emma bounded off the porch and raced toward Ethan, her hand clenched tightly around the black box. She handed it to Ethan.

He opened it, and the ring sparkled in the sunlight. He took it out and bent down on one knee. "Olivia Daniels, will you marry me?"

With Ethan on his knee and Emma looking up to her, Olivia wept as she said, "Yes, I'll marry you." She kneeled on the grass as Ethan placed the ring on her finger. They kissed, and when they looked up, they saw the halo of the mid-afternoon sun framing the angel between them.

CHAPTER 36

The cool October breezes off of Lake Huron did little to lessen the warmth in the hearts of those in attendance at the wedding of Olivia Daniels and Ethan Stone. The late afternoon sun shone brightly as Pastor Carlton officiated with the lighthouse in full splendor behind him. With the music playing, Emma, in her sparkling white dress and with a red ribbon in her hair, started the procession with a bouquet of white roses from Ethan's garden. Ethan leaned down to give her a kiss when she reached her spot at the front.

In her gleaming white gown, Olivia held the arm of her father as they walked down the aisle. Her smile was just as big as Ethan's.

After Mr. Daniels gave his daughter a kiss, he stood tall to Ethan and whispered, "Take good care of her."

Ethan winked and smiled. "I will. I promise."

Ethan took Olivia by the hand, and her grasp told him she was never letting go.

Once Olivia and Ethan said "I do" and Ethan kissed his bride, the party moved to the Daniels' B&B for the reception in the newly renovated barn. People marveled at the beauty of the wood and the lights that shone in all of the right places.

"Did I tell you how beautiful you look today?" Ethan said, holding his bride close to him as they danced in the glow of the spotlight.

"I think you might have mentioned it once or twice."

Olivia's smile radiated the joy in her heart. "I might add that you look particularly handsome in your tux."

He grinned and kissed her gently on the forehead. "A certain someone helped me pick it out. She said it would make me look dashing."

Olivia laughed. They both looked over and saw Emma sitting with her best friend Bella. She noticed they were looking at her, and she responded by blowing a kiss to both of them.

"She is something, Ethan."

"That she is. I don't know whether I'd be standing here with you right now if she hadn't shown up on my doorstep that Friday night. She led me back to church, and then she led me back to you."

"And God brought us together."

"For good this time."

Olivia let Ethan's strong arms envelop her. She felt so safe and cared for. She was home. She looked around at the smiling faces and then the beautiful barn. "And this place looks absolutely fabulous, Ethan. You did amazing work."

Ethan shrugged. "It was all my boss's idea. She's very demanding."

Olivia chuckled. "Is that so?"

"Yeah. She's a stern taskmaster."

"How do you put up with her?"

Ethan rested his forehead against Olivia's. "Faith, hope, and love."

Olivia raised her head, the tears of happiness forming in her eyes. "But the greatest is love."

THE END

Rob Shumaker is an attorney living in Danville, Illinois. *The Angel Between Them* is his first Christian romance novel. He is also the author of *Turning the Page*, *Christmas in Huron Cove*, and *Learning to Love Again*, the second, third, and fourth books in the Huron Cove Series.

Did you enjoy *The Angel Between Them*? Readers like you can make a big difference. Reviews are powerful tools to attract more readers so I can continue to write engaging stories that people enjoy.

If you enjoyed the book, I would be grateful if you could write an honest review (as short or as long as you like) on your favorite book retailer.

Thank you and happy reading.

Rob Shumaker

To join my newsletter and to receive updates on new releases and exclusive bonus content, go to

www.RobShumakerBooks.com

... .—

Made in the USA
Middletown, DE
04 December 2021